MW01641763

THE TAKING OF AGNÈS

THE TAKING OF AGNÈS

JENNIFER POTTER

JONATHAN CAPE
THIRTY BEDFORD SQUARE LONDON

First published 1985

Jonathan Cape Ltd, 30 Bedford Square, London WC1B 3EL

British Library Cataloguing in Publication Data

Potter, Jennifer
The taking of Agnès.
I. Title
823'.914[F] PR6066.077/

ISBN 0-224-02281-4

The author and publishers would like to thank New Directions Publishing Corporation for permission to reproduce the poem from *Configurations* by Octavio Paz.

Photoset in Great Britain by
Rowland Phototypesetting Ltd, Bury St Edmunds, Suffolk
and printed by St Edmundsbury Press
Bury St Edmunds, Suffolk

For A.M.P. and J.B.P.

You will have to learn . . . that in this part of the world there is nothing to do but to plant cane and cocoa, and make rum, and cultivate tobacco, – or open a magazine for the sale of Madras handkerchiefs and foulards, – and eat, drink, sleep, perspire.

Lafcadio Hearn, *Two Years in the French West Indies*, 1890

The wind has risen early tonight. It catches the outhouse door which bangs open and shut, while urgent voices in the trees betoken rain. Thank God the time for hurricanes is past.

Plantation Ste Croix
St Antoine
Martinique

3 January

Dear Agnès,
You want me to come home. My answer is that having lived on this island for the past thirty-five years of my adult life I am too old to subscribe to notions of a home existing other than where I am.

Your affectionate aunt,
Alicia.

The rain inches up the valley. When it strikes my house on the edge of the plantation it cuts off the noises of the jungle and the insects which plague my life: an unsavoury alliance of cicadas, cockroaches, spiders, centipedes, and members of the ant family, some of which are said to bring good luck.

I think rather they may crawl upon me at night and catch me unawares.

11 rue de l'Alboni
Paris 16

29 January

Dear Aunt Lily,
The family insist. Father called them to Paris at the weekend. The papers are full of the most frightful rumours of revolt, and that business with the riots makes us fear for your safety.

Charles did most of the talking. Do you remember him? He ran a construction company in Lille and now works for a merchant bank with interests on the island. Informants tell him that international agitators have been sighted in Fort de France. That can only mean trouble. His wife Madeleine was there, sober as a mouse, and Uncle Antoine who annoyed Maman with stories of the War. I'm not sure which one. I think he's senile. And Florence and Guy and your cousin Rudolphe – they all share father's concern and have decided to act before it's too late. I've been asked to bring you back to France. They also think a change will do me good. I'm under a cloud. Just a little one. So I kiss you and look forward to seeing you very soon. You'll be happy here, I know.

More kisses,
Agnès.

We are inside the rain now: myself, Eveline and her daughter Yvette, unless the child runs wild in the forest. I distrust Yvette heartily and have warned Eveline more than once that without closer supervision she will come to no good. The child is one of several matters about which we disagree. Personally I never venture out to the plantation after the sun has set. It is a wild and lonely place, full of strange shadows that speak of misdeeds.

Plantation Ste Croix
St Antoine
Martinique

14 February

Dear Agnès,
You must appreciate that in pursuit of their own interests the newspapers are prone to exaggerate. One small riot caused, I understand, by a parking dispute in which the uniformed police were foolish enough to get involved hardly constitutes a revolution. Believe me, Agnès, I know the people well enough to recognise their capabilities. They do not like us but that dislike will never be translated into acts of wilful violence. Our dealings are circumscribed by habits of politeness born of our common education, and parricide is not one of their virtues. This is France after all. The people vote in the same elections as we do; they pay their taxes and receive their benefits. By this I mean that they are Frenchmen. Black Frenchmen, perhaps, but in every other respect the same as you or I. The troubles will pass as they have always done.

Your loving aunt,
Alicia.

P.S. I do not think that a man once publicly condemned, as Charles was, for selling reinforced concrete at exorbitant profit can properly be said to have his ear to the ground.

The rain clatters on the roof and streaks in a block from the gable, anaesthetising the landscape. The sound comforts me, and brings to mind my Great Aunt Mathilde, an eminent lepidopterist who charted the species of the Rio Negro. Since her disappearance in Brazil I have always mistrusted the jungle as if I feared hacking my way through the lianas to discover Aunt Matty, still alive, oblivious to the intervening years. The reality is somewhat different. There are many ways to die in a rain forest. Nevertheless her presumed fate explains why I prefer my nature tamed and labelled in the Jardin des Plantes where I can admire without discomfort the giant tree ferns and graceful vistas. Having elected to live in a tropical island does not force me to endure its peculiar indignities.

11 rue de l'Alboni
Paris 16

1 March

My dear Alicia,
Agnès has shown me your last letter. As your brother and head of the family I implore you to listen to reason. When you stand at the centre of events it is not easy to assume the correct perspective. The 'small riot' you talk of left three people dead and caused considerable damage to property. Banaszeuc at the Ministry informed me personally that the figure may run to

several million francs. We are therefore preparing a house for you on the edge of our estates near Verdun where your independence is guaranteed. The house has two simple bedrooms – very clean – and a small kitchen and bathroom. The comfortable though moderately-sized sitting-room has fine views over the plains. It was previously occupied by my overseer and his wife, an excellent housekeeper. When you return you will recognise that we have acted in your best interests and that your place is with us in the land of your ancestors.

I embrace you in the name of the family,
Gustave.

Plantation Ste Croix
St Antoine
Martinique

8 March

Dear Gustave,
Your offer, most kindly intended, must be declined. I have lost the taste for your landscape and can no longer deposit my baggage beneath your dismal skies. I do not mean to be rude. When André first brought me to these islands I nourished the illusion that I would one day return. I know myself better now and whatever illusions subsist will remain with me until I die, which shall be here, I assure you, and in my bed like a good Christian.

Forgive me, Gustave, and accept my grateful thanks for your offer. That I am moved to reject it demonstrates nothing more than the obstinacy of an old woman who wishes to remain in peace. I, too, embrace you in the name of the family and hope that this correspondence may cease. There are plenty of other subjects about which I would gladly converse.

Your loving Alicia.

It is quiet now and if it were daytime a rainbow would move slowly across the water. I think rainbows are rare in France, at least on the northern plains among the orchards and the battlefields where my brother wishes to transport me.

André would understand, but he cannot plead my cause as he lies in the white-tiled graveyard, under palm trees which bring him neither comfort nor shade, trapped between the third and fourth generations of a slave economy. His next door neighbour, Nestor Deriab, worked as a postman, which exemplifies the extent of our democracy. I visit André at all major Catholic feast days and at some of my own, knowing I cannot bring myself to leave him, untended, to the cupidity of malevolent spirits with different coloured faces from our own.

I was married to André for twenty years until he died one day of the fever. He had spent the morning in the cane fields, came home at noon complaining of a chill, was dead within a week. They say that only strangers succumb; that the blood of men born on the island is protected with magical ingredients, a marvellous antidote to these wasting climes. They are wrong, my friends, always wrong. Never subscribe to their tales or you will end up living with ghosts.

From the kitchen I hear the growl of Eveline's singing like a *café dansant* at the edge of the jungle, and the slamming of a door which must be the child, Yvette, going in or out.

Adieu madras, adieu foulards
Adieu rob'soie et colliers-choux
Doudou à moin li ka pa-ti
Hélas, hélas c'est pou toujou.

She sings her limited repertory in a curious mixture of French and patois, always at night after the rains have passed. Her voice, which cannot be described as tuneful, nevertheless pinches my soul, and I would dearly love her to cease but have not the heart to ask.

From my veranda I smell flowers in the fresh darkness. I must sleep soon. It is late.

TO ALICIA MONTFORT DE SAINTE CROIX
ARRIVE FORT DE FRANCE 18 MARCH AF 636 11.30 HRS
STOP SORRY STOP AGNÈS

1

MY NIECE, Agnès Montfort, arrived on the 18th of March and in the short time she stayed on this island conquered a number of hearts on account of her slate-grey eyes, untidy blonde hair, a skin translucent like a child's and the quickness of her laughter. After thirty-eight days she disappeared, apparently kidnapped by the *Santanistes*, a group of angry dreamers who orchestrate their protests like the guard dogs in my valley, chained to the wall and baying at the moon.

That the *Santanistes* took Agnès – and were therefore entirely to blame for what happened – is the official version of events which deems my niece the innocent victim of political forces outside her control or understanding. Knowing her better than our somewhat short-sighted officials I consider the matter a little more complicated than their tidy theory presumes: a victim, perhaps, but as for innocence . . .

The only certainty is that Agnès has gone, leaving behind the echo of her laughter which even now calls from empty rooms. I open doors and search in hidden corners but nothing stirs in the polished stillness. Looking for Agnès has become a habit, like judging the likelihood of rain from the clouds stacked above Mont Pelée or the haze which rises off the sugar cane.

I miss her dreadfully, in spite of everything.

Searching for some disregarded clue I move through the cool, dark house, into the sitting-room at the front which is surrounded on two sides by verandas and looks across well-tended lawns to the cassia trees and the plantation beyond. It is a fine room though bare of the objects you might expect: my crystal glasses, the Dresden figurines, all the bric-à-brac of a woman past fifty. They were smashed, my pretty things, and are quite irreplaceable. No matter. You shall not find me sad.

I continue through the house, into André's study which remains much as he left it: its paintwork tinged with age and tobacco smoke, his maps of the island and our lands adorning the wall behind the heavy oak desk from which he ran our affairs with good intentions but marginal success. I find neither Agnès nor her echo. Along the corridor her room is quite deserted. It once belonged to Angeline, the prettiest of André's sisters, who exerted such a terrible fascination over Agnès. My niece is absent, of course.

More quickly I retrace my steps through the house, into the bathroom with its frieze of fleur-de-lis tiles above the window, the small parlour (rarely used), the kitchen at the back overlooking a ragged cluster of banana trees, the washroom which smells of clean linen and pressed flowers. I am driven by the spectre of Agnès like a *loupgarou* in the mountains.

The third stair creaks as it has always done. At the top I pause outside Eveline's room, reassured by the sound of her quaint conversations. The child must be with her: little Yvette with the face and manners of a monkey.

In the two spare bedrooms I stop myself looking under the beds and go instead into my own room where I throw open the shutters, releasing sharp sunlight that hurts my eyes. To the north Mont Pelée is obscured by clouds which stretch eastwards across the horizon, skimming close to the sea, while in the distance a dog's howl is answered by another then another, up and down the valley, creating a desultory cacophony that chills my heart.

When Eveline hears the dogs calling at night she crosses herself and mutters snatches of incomprehensible magic: there is evil, she swears, the devils roam. I humour her childish beliefs and have on occasions caught myself imitating her actions – though that is behind me now. I mark the sign of the cross in church, where it belongs, and the rest of the time converse with devils which have dwelt here since Agnès disappeared.

This record represents my only chance of salvation, my only hope finally to silence their chatterings. They are a noisy lot, these demons, and spiteful, delighting in setting me traps and snapping at my heels. Their constant babblings bind me to the spectre of past events, though why things happen, and how, I wish I knew. You see, we were all implicated in one way or another: myself, Claude, Agnès, David Taverner. Each of us guilty, but who must bear the greatest share of blame? Only I can tell, my devils whisper cunningly. Only I can piece together the scraps of evidence in my possession: Agnès's diary, the notes she wrote in the hills with the *Santanistes*, reports laboriously compiled by my detective. They make me a judge when I was but a witness and we have sworn a pact in which I offer up my truth in exchange for silence. They are damnable task-masters, believe me. Nothing is ever neatly black or white, a lesson quickly learnt in these islands which devised precise definitions for all the shades of colour between Europe and Africa. When I am finished they must keep their promises and let me be at peace.

An exorcism and also an epitaph – to love, to dreams, a better life I might have known. It should be dedicated to Claude though I cannot quite bring myself to write his name on the fly-leaf. I know now that I never understood him correctly. Like all of us his actions had unfortunate consequences. But his heart, where was that lodged? I cannot tell. I have his poems (lamentably obscure), his recent letter from Durango, and a host of memories that reveal nothing about what he felt, in his heart.

David Taverner, the Englishman, has also deserted me so I cannot seek out his opinion. From the way I treated him that is hardly surprising. At moments of stress he had the habit of playing an imaginary piano in thin air which drove me to distraction. 'Dear sir,' I would say, 'kindly keep your hands to yourself.' Like all Englishmen his heart is muddied with conflicting emotions. I think he fell in love with Agnès after she disappeared and I find a certain justice in that.

Far below my window darkening clouds sweep in across the Atlantic and a thick band of surf denotes the limit of the bay. We live at the mercy of the elements; they underline the fact that our residence is temporary and all who come here are strangers of one sort or another: the slaves, indentured Indians and men and women from the *métropole* who administer a surly populace with little love and much less understanding. Yet the people forget that without French brains and French money the entire edifice would crumble and slip back unnoticed into our savage seas. Freedom, indeed. As if that commodity can be bought and sold in the market place and as if, in the end, it makes the slightest difference to our happiness.

My friend Achille Gonstran, mayor of St Antoine, would doubtless disagree as he believes with the utmost sincerity that France must rule no more. At times he gives the impression of crying – great tears well up in the corners of his eyes – which partly explains his charm although the origin of this phenomenon is surely physiological, unless black men cry more easily than we do.

Quite often these days I call in at the *mairie*, an insignificant building overlooking St Antoine's dusty square, behind the statue of Schoelcher which adorns each commune on the island to commemorate the abolition of slavery. In St Antoine his alabaster head is sandwiched between the *mairie*, the war memorial and the church, a pretty building with a red-tiled roof and French colonial spire situated across from the post office on the opposite side of the square. The arrangement is, one might say, convenient. One may conduct one's official business and post one's letters before making peace with God.

At my last visit Gonstran's secretary attempted to bring order to the abundance of paperwork spread about his cramped office in this forgotten outpost of municipal government. Gonstran clutched at his papers blown about the room by the erratic action of an antiquated fan that picks up speed occasionally and threatens to cast off from the ceiling, as if the power has been miraculously increased.

One of the items his secretary wished to throw away – which he gave instead to me – was a copy of the poster of Agnès which, after she went missing, was stuck to every noticeboard on the island. I had to take it though it seemed a tactless gesture from so considerate a man.

Agnès smiled at me radiantly over a bare, tanned shoulder, her eyes puckered by sunlight, and behind her the wild ocean. Strands of blonde hair swept across her forehead as she threw back her head in the wind. This image, captured by David Taverner, is the one I treasure most because she was so evidently happy, smiling at the Englishman with all the seductive charms of her twenty years. An enchantress, you might say, who brought life and laughter to my quiet house among the trees before slowly, imperceptibly, the laughter gave way to lies and trickery, by which time we were powerless to prevent what happened because she had ensnared us all.

2

THE EVENTS surrounding the disappearance of my niece began several months before she arrived. I can even supply a precise day, the 15th of November, when I was deputed to welcome Claude Cerda at Fort de France international airport on behalf of the island's Committee for Cultural Co-operation. This honour had been bitterly contested by Madame Ségovie who claimed that as she was black and as her husband was Secretary-General of the Union of Proletarian Workers she had more fitting credentials to greet a poet of the revolution. (She lost the argument. And whatever workers exist on this island they do not constitute a proletariat.)

Heartened by my victory, I arrived at the airport with a bouquet of red hibiscus picked that morning from my garden on the edge of the plantation, which I offered first to an aeronautical engineer from Toulouse and by the time I realised my mistake Claude stood alone by the exit, a little stouter than I had imagined, not so tall. I walked towards him and thrust the flowers into his outstretched hand. He beamed at me, a cross between a peasant and a priest, his face illuminated with a fierce pride.

'Allow me to present myself,' he said in his beautiful Spanish voice, bowing deeply from the waist, 'Claude Arturo Cerda Santiago.'

'Oh dear. Have I got the right man? I was supposed to meet a Señor Cerda. A poet.'

He snapped the flowers away in his suitcase and, standing to attention, said, 'Santiago is my mother's name. It is where I was born and the battlecry of the conquistadores. For me it is, well, logical.'

He gave me his arm and we passed together through the automatic doors which had been opening and shutting throughout our introduction. By the car he bowed again with a flourish and insisted on unlocking the doors. I could not immediately find the key – he held me still by the elbow – and I knew I acted like a foolish girl. At last we were settled, and Claude talked animatedly as we drove to the house by the sea which our Committee had prepared for his stay. He told me of his hopes, and his daughters, and the poems he would write as our guest, assuming I could follow the leaps and somersaults of his imagination.

If he noticed my silence he was much too polite to comment. I laughed at his exuberant spirits, nervously at first, having lost the habit, then more freely as the strength of his presence teased out my responses, and I found myself stealing glances at him while he looked the other way. I must have blushed at many things he said, feeling young again, and full of hope.

To spite Madame Ségovie I asked him to dine with me that night, the first of many such occasions. When he entered the house, he looked about him and walked straight to André's chair where he sat down without further ceremony. It was quite uncanny. I could not ask him to move and took my place meekly at his side, elated to hear a man's voice again, resonant, assured of mastering my humble world.

After dinner I played him my mazurkas to camouflage the sound of Eveline's singing. He called me Our Lady of the Waltzes and I loved him a little from the start.

They all arrived with flowers, even David Taverner the Englishman who, according to the mayor, flew in with the Gaillard brothers and a cargo of orchids bound for Dominica, though why he could not enter the island by the proper channels, like everyone else, remains a mystery.

Wedged between the orchid crates and the window he watched the shadow glide across the landscape: scrubland and mangrove swamps to the south, the mountains of Vauclin, the plains of Lamentin shaded green and gold from the sugar cane, the rocky coastline to the north with stark black sand, the forest by the shadow of the volcano.

The small plane jolted to a stop outside a disused hangar bearing the remnants of a painted sign long since washed away or blistered in the sun. Suspecting he might have landed in the wrong place the poor fellow needed encouragement from the pilots that this was indeed his destination. The door was opened and a blast of hot air hit him in the face. He stared at the coconut palms dotted about the airfield's perimeter, and the heat haze which burnt off the runway. After a second or two he jumped down to the tarmac and watched the plane taxi to the end of the runway then roar back towards him at full throttle, forcing him to step aside as it took off for Dominica.

The rest of Taverner's arrival I heard from Léopold who drives around the island in a battered black Peugeot and who had been dispatched by a contact to meet the Englishman at the airport. Either the Gaillard brothers flew in early or Léopold was late – he had stopped to collect some friends, his co-conspirator Gaspard and a serious girl called Christophine who wears glasses and speaks little, at least in my presence. When they arrived Taverner sat perfectly still on the grass, in the full heat of the sun. I believe this because I doubt whether Léopold, who was born in Santo Domingo, shares our incredulity at the madness of dogs and Englishmen. He parked the Peugeot in the safety of the shadows.

The sound of the door slamming disturbed the young Englishman who stood up as Léopold walked towards him. Maybe he thought there was something odd about Léopold who has a penchant for dark glasses, calypso shirts and vulgar gold rings which shine dully against the blackness of his skin. Whatever it was, Léopold found himself staring down the barrel of a gun which Taverner pulled from his case and waved – apologetically – at Léopold's chest. Taverner is the only man I know who can handle a weapon as if it were something else.

Léopold laughed, or so he claims, and the Englishman put away his pistol. From that moment the two struck up an improbable friendship, the taciturn Englishman whom Agnès fancifully suggested might have been a spy, and mad Léopold who has taken to calling at my house, unbidden, and installing himself on my veranda. He says I owe him money and if I did not know him better I would think he threatened me.

The flowers Agnès brought were simply those of youth, packed away in her baggage with the innocence of her twenty years.

She sailed through the customs barrier, flung her arms around me though we had not met since she lay in her mother's arms, gave me a present (a travelling clock, beautifully gift-wrapped and tied with blue ribbons, a logical gift had I the slightest intention of returning home to France), and from the moment she arrived never ceased to battle with my silence.

'Papa sends his love and looks forward to your return . . . Maman says she will take you shopping, as soon as you arrive . . . It will be cold, so cold . . . Cousin Rudolphe has planned an excursion . . . You *must* show me the island,' she paused for breath and looked about her, glowing with abundant good health. 'Simone says it's beautiful – she's my friend, my best friend. I've many friends in Paris. I think I'll love it here too. It's like an adventure.'

Everything, for Agnès, was an adventure: the warm, conservatory smell of earth after the rain has passed, name tags on trees in the Jardin des Plantes, dead dogs by the roadside, and frightened bandits in the hills.

Once I had disentangled myself from her embrace, I stepped back to look at her more closely. The girl was quite devastating and it was hard to believe Gustave (a correct and rather gloomy man) capable of producing such a deadly specimen. From her mother Agnès had doubtless inherited her striking good looks which she carried carelessly, unaware of their effect on others, but neither parent could account for her height or the loose-limbed walk with which she paraded her confidence in life and all it owed her. This child, who marvelled at every change in the landscape, and the gilded light, reminded me of the woman I had been when I first arrived as a bride.

On the windward coast we stopped to admire the ocean. Strong warm winds roar across the surf, filling your head with thunder as they drive the clouds westwards over the mountain.

'You'll really miss it when you come back with me to France,' Agnès shouted above the wind.

'I have no intention of leaving.'

'But Father insists . . .'

'Gustave is my brother. He shall not rule my life.'

'He'll be furious. That's why I've come here. And think of all they've done: the house, the preparations . . .' She hugged me impulsively and left the sentence unfinished.

It was a conversation we were to repeat many times and though Agnès spied on me for Gustave when it occurred to her, appearing suddenly in doorways and questioning me about my plans for departure, I could not hold this against her.

To Eveline's delight she filled the house with laughter and trailed in her wake a stream of hopeful young men, sons of my neighbours who arrived with flowers and bright conversations, as well as the Englishman drawn by chance into our circle, and Claude my dearest friend. We none of us noticed the storm clouds which should have heralded the arrival of Agnès into our quiet lives.

3

Agnès sits at the table by her open window writing furiously in the black leather diary fastened with a golden clasp, the diary in which she recorded her impressions of the landscape – no more than usually banal – and drew sharp little snapshots of acquaintances and friends whom she collected as Great Aunt Mathilde had collected butterflies, disinfected with formaldehyde and pierced with a pin through the heart.

Friends of the Ste Croix family remarked on Agnès's resemblance to André's younger sister, Angeline. The one was dark and the other fair but otherwise they were passably similar. People remembered also the stories whispered about Angeline – that she had never died, and here was Agnès to prove them right.

'Why do people stare at me, Aunt Lily?'

'Because you're white, I expect.'

'White people stare at me too.'

'Then you must remind them of someone.'

'Someone I know?'

'No. She would be old now, as I am.'

'You're not old, Aunt Lily. Who was she?'

'A girl called Angeline.'

'André's sister?'

'That's right, my dear. And may I remind you not to call me Lily.'

'Was she pretty, this Angeline?'

'I believe so.'

'You don't seem certain.'

'No. And never mention her name. Not here, in my household.'

'Why ever not? She was your sister-in-law.'

'I have my reasons.'

'What sort of reasons?'

'It was a long time ago.'

'An eternity?' Agnès tossed back her head and laughed. 'Anyway, I've seen her photograph and she *was* pretty, I know.'

'Why ask, if you know the answer?'

Agnès knew already how to hurt me. She had an instinct for divining my weakest spot and pressing home the blade. And what can children know about eternity?

19 March

Aunt Lily is quite terrifying but I love her dearly and do so want her to like me too. She must have been very beautiful once, in a classic sort of way. Still is, of course, but there's something about her which suggests she's been touched up:

her beautiful dark brown hair with auburn lights that are almost too auburn; her clothes, always so neat and clean – heaven knows how she manages it in this heat; her elegant face impeccably made-up, never a smudge or a drop of sweat. She's like a ballerina with exquisite taste who makes you feel overweight, badly dressed and much too tall. I'm sure she's only a year or two younger than Papa so she must be fifty, at least. She would even put Maman in the shade.

Today she took me to visit her friend Señor Cerda who has rubbed shoulders (so she claims) with Fidel Castro and may have met Guevara in the jungle – not the sort of credentials I would have thought she appreciated. He reminded me of a prosperous banker, flashing a mouth full of gold teeth and wearing an expensive though slightly ragged suit in spite of the heat. He speaks with a thick Spanish accent so that talking to him is extremely hard work except for the initiated (Aunt Lily) and even when I hear properly he seems to talk in riddles. Perhaps that's because he's a poet.

We sat on his balcony: Aunt Lily looking regal in the rocking chair (the seat of honour), the 'great man' in a deckchair, myself on the steps. Out of the blue Señor Cerda announced – to me, I think – that he experienced a nostalgia for crossroads. God knows what he meant. That he was born a gypsy? That he liked making choices? That he collected signposts? When I agreed with him he laughed and said, 'Mademoiselle is a pretty girl, non?' which made Aunt Lily cross. They understand each other perfectly though they don't say much but communicate by sign language, a nod of the head, a slight wave of the hand, long pauses in which they smile at each other like conspirators. I feel definitely *de trop*.

The house smells of garlic and sugar and vanilla. I lie in bed and listen to the storms.

20 March

Uncle André stands rather stiffly on the cabinet beside Aunt Lily's bed. A young man in uniform, terribly dashing, with a clipped moustache and the hint of a smile behind his raffish eyes. I hope he wasn't Vichy like everyone else. We took him flowers in the cemetery by the sea, frangipani for the uncle I've never seen. Aunt Lily talked to him when she thought I wasn't looking, a conversation that consisted mainly of brain teasers with suitable pauses for his replies. He must be a remarkable ghost.

21 March

Through the jalousies of my room I look out at shady trees and beyond them the wild, sad plantation. I feel I was born to live here. The island is more beautiful than anything I've ever known, so peaceful and strange, in spite of the many things to remind me of home like signs for Electricité de France framed against a jungle skyline. This may be France but it's hardly Europe which makes the displacement more real, somehow, and certainly more bewildering.

Señor Cerda came for supper. He was very excitable and his conversation ran all over the place. We could only sit and listen. He told jokes about his revolutionary friends, Castro and the like, and laughed before he'd finished so we rarely heard an ending. He seemed a different man from the other day. Fiery and really quite alarming, banging his fist on the table without a thought for the china. Aunt Lily was very deferential and gave him enough to feed an army. Somehow it all disappeared between the jokes. When she was out of the room he said I should visit him one day to hear his poems. I agreed and he smiled and said my hair was like moonstones. Then he laughed so much he almost choked. I couldn't see what was funny but I like him. He's weird. Aunt

Lily wore a lilac silk dress and looked like a duchess except she smelt of mothballs.

22 March
Pale sunrise. I get up when the cocks crow and feel something magic about the light, so much better than the lurid sunsets which squeeze every possible drama out of the sky and are followed by dusk, then blackness. Eveline says that at the time of the full moon it's best to carry an umbrella, as you can suffer from moonstroke. I wonder what Señor Cerda makes of it all; I expect he's terribly wise.

23 March
The more Aunt Lily tells me of my uncle, the more I like him. Apparently he wanted to be an explorer and collected maps which hang in his study; maps of the plantation and Martinique and places he'd never visited, all hung together without any order. I'm sure he understood about crossroads. Aunt Lily says he grew sugar when he should have grown bananas and switched to coffee just before the blight. They nearly went bankrupt several times and even when he grew the right crop at the right time it was flattened by the tail end of a hurricane. But he was quite at home with the stars.

Uncle André's sisters: Sophie, Maryse and Angeline. They sit in the photograph under the shade of a *fromager*, wide skirts spread about them on the grass and behind them their brother standing to attention dressed in shorts and a tropical hat. Little Sophie, small, dark and vivacious, drowned in the Rivière St Jacques. Plain, good-hearted Maryse, the last of them to go. And Angeline, sweet Angeline with jet black hair and a perfectly oval face. She haunts me, perhaps because in certain lights we're meant to look like each other. Something about our eyes, apparently, and the way we stare at people. Maman's always trying to get me to stop. She thinks it's brazen but I can't help it. In the photograph Angeline's eyes are cold, clear, and somehow fragile. She looks as if she knows what she wants and intends to get it, without any fuss, because it's her right. Aunt Lily refused to talk about her. Said the girl had always been 'sick' (by which I think she meant sick in the head). She stamped her foot and flounced out of the room and I knew I'd said the wrong thing again.

24 March

Went by *taxi collectif* to Fort de France driven by one of the blackest men I've ever seen and absolutely enormous. He could hardly bend himself over the steering wheel. I expect he comes from Haiti. He drove impossibly fast and I shut my eyes for most of the journey, shaken about with the other passengers who talked among themselves in patois and looked at me coldly as if I had no right to be there. Met Claude in the bookshop and drank beer with him in a café off the Savane. Conversation even more oblique than usual. He told me of a statue he owns, the head of a goddess, and I couldn't for the life of me understand why. We laughed a lot and he talked of his daughters, Rose and Isobella. At least I think they're his daughters. Aunt Lily wanted to know what had kept me so long. I didn't mention our meeting because I felt she might disapprove.

In the afternoon I was introduced to Olivier d'Aurigny who came to tea with his mother. That says it all. He's really rather sweet with curly fair hair, soft like a boy's and a smile that made me want to put my arm round him because he looks so young and trusting. His mother, having looked me over a few times, obviously decided I would make a suitable companion for her son because she suggested very pointedly that the 'young people' might like to go out one night for dinner. Olivier turned red and mumbled some half-baked invitation. I had to agree. She looks the kind of woman who usually gets her way.

I wish Louis would write to me soon. He promised to write at least twice a week, even more if he could get the time. I left his photograph behind and have almost forgotten what he looks like.

25 March

Wherever I go I feel, deep down, that I've been here before. We drive through the cane fields or up mountain roads and I know exactly what we'll see when we turn the corner. I'm always right, that's the strange part, like a ghost coming home. Even faces are familiar and I have the weird feeling of picking up conversations started much earlier with total strangers. In brighter moments I think I'm mad but no one else notices. I could describe their grandmothers and they wouldn't think me odd. Not a bit. The old ones shake their heads and talk of Angeline as if she were my friend, which she is of course except we never met. Her secrets obsess me, like the daughter everyone denies. Mme d'Aurigny had a fit when I asked what happened to the girl. Eyes like vipers, she fanned herself furiously with a newspaper and announced very haughtily that the dead deserve our respect, whatever their faults, and that I wasn't to mention it to my aunt. Silly old bag. It's none of her business. Yet Eveline insists the story is true. After making me swear some complicated oath she took me to see the child's grave in a far corner of the estate only we got lost and Eveline became convinced the spirits were leading us a dance because she'd let loose one of their secrets. We tramped round in circles, Eveline saying her rosary loudly and rather shakily, until we came to the hurricane shelter, a low, windowless building almost strangled by thick, vicious-looking creepers. I went in alone. Eveline said it was haunted. (I suspect the truth is much more mundane. The place was almost habitable – it had the trappings of furniture and an outsize crucifix above the door. But who could live in a house without windows?) Perhaps Eveline does know something because when I crossed the threshold I felt the place was waiting for someone. That it was haunted not by the dead but by the living. For once I was really scared. I stood there among the leaves which had blown through the door, cut off from the sunlight, and felt a shiver of evil. We came home after that without finding the grave. I felt unspeakably cold and Eveline was half out of her wits. Aunt Lily was waiting for us and demanded to know why we had been walking in the sun. I didn't tell her. When she's in one of those moods there's a hardness about her, like a flint in the heart.

26 March

Near the house I stumbled into Yvette playing with clay dolls arranged in a circle. When I called her name she froze to the spot, like stone, staring at me very coldly. The dolls had large ugly heads with slits for eyes and I've seen them in dreams. It must be Yvette who spies on me in the plantation. I know there's someone there though I can't see them. Branches crack behind me and when I stop they stop, slinking into the undergrowth. Aunt Lily said it was my imagination – the effect of too much sun, or a fever – then she gave herself away by admitting that even the trees have eyes.

27 March

Never smell the flowers you give to Our Lady or you steal from her soul. The lights you see darting at night across the mountain: Père Labat's ghost, the werewolves, a solitary Jew. (I've seen Chinamen here, and strange mixed bloods, but never the trace of a Jew.) Aimée Dubuc de Rivery, born at Le Robert, captured by barbary pirates and carried off to the Grand Turk who made her his consort; like Josephine she became more than a queen. This place breeds legends and wills you to believe them as Eveline does, with all her heart. Only Aunt Lily is unmoved as if anxious to remain a permanent spectator of her own life. She told me the story of St Pierre, little Paris of the West Indies, without once commenting on the sadness of it all. She might have been reciting a shopping list. Yet a city died beneath the volcano, thirty thousand souls – the entire population destroyed except for Auguste Ciparis, a condemned prisoner kept below ground under sentence of death. The dead man lived while the others died – there must be a moral in that.

I can't believe how stupid they were. Mt Pelée had been erupting for days, covering the streets with fine white ash. A factory was engulfed by boiling mud and most of the trees in the Jardin des Plantes turned brown and died. The Governor of Martinique marshalled his troops to keep the population in place at least until after the elections which were bitterly contested by both the Radicals (blacks) and the Progressives (whites). Each side claimed Pelée's eruption as a sign in its favour.

A scientific Commission of Enquiry set up by the ruling whites declared the town perfectly safe, devoting most of its report to the unfortunate fate of the trees in the Jardin des Plantes. Three days before the second ballot everyone was dead, except Ciparis, of course, and he wasn't entitled to vote. Claude says that some men are blind to warnings, even when they blanket their streets like snow. I think that, at least, is true.

28 March

Aunt Lily is determined not to return to France, a decision I respect but Father insists and I'm here for a purpose after all. I'm not sure why he's so set on her return. He can't be after her money because we're richer than she is. I broached the subject again when she took me to visit her 'stones' which she keeps in a clearing near the house. Aunt Lily said she wasn't a parcel to be shipped around the world at her relatives' convenience.

The stones are pre-Columbian and if they're Gods they're horribly cheerful ones, scratched with childlike drawings of little men with pumpkin heads and a few strands of hair standing on end. Aunt Lily was angry when I said they looked like golliwogs and warned me never to repeat that in public. I wish I didn't offend her so easily. I do my best which clearly isn't enough.

29 March

Peuple noir, pouvoir blanc painted in huge red letters on a banner hung from the mast at the top of the radio station and no one knows how it got there. Aunt Lily says it means trouble and thinks I should leave. I suppose she just wants to be rid of me.

30 March

Sunset. I stand with Claude on the warm black sand before his house. Nearby a fisherman mends his nets under the palm trees. His boat is called *Seigneur de l'Univers*. We look at the red and orange sky. 'It's very beautiful,' I venture at last. Claude turns towards me and puts his hand on mine, saying with a solemn smile, 'I'm very touched, Mademoiselle, that you notice such things.' (I was merely thinking of something to say.) He takes hold of my hand and looks deep into my eyes until I feel dizzy and have to turn away.

31 March
At Josephine's museum Olivier d'Aurigny showed me a letter from Napoleon, a love letter in which he complained petulantly that she was neglecting him. You could hear the whine in his voice and I suspect he was a very unpleasant little man. We walked hand in hand through the ruined distillery and sat on the grass behind a bed of canna lilies. I only wish he was older. In a couple of years I'd fall for him completely. We returned by the coast road, stopping for a time at Anses d'Arlets, and I got home to a letter from Louis. He had met Simone for tea at the Coupole and talked of nothing but me. Then they drove out for dinner at Fontainebleau and he swears that he can't get me out of his mind. We'll see about that.

1 April
Aunt Lily left early to do some shopping in Fort de France and as soon as she'd left I went into her room which smells of old-fashioned roses. In a wooden chest I found all her fine clothes, the lilac dress she wore for Claude and a long white ball gown stitched all over with the most perfect embroidery. It fitted me exactly which is very odd as we're completely different sizes. The desk wasn't locked. I felt terribly

guilty but if she was more open about things I wouldn't need to creep around like this.

I had hoped to discover the secret of Angeline and her daughter – find a birth certificate or a marriage licence – anything to tell me what happened. Not a thing, though enough about André to write a book. I did find a photograph of my aunt as a young woman. The photographer had cropped her below the shoulders, completely bare so you might think she wasn't wearing any clothes, just a single strand of pearls and that proud pointed face with its arched eyebrows and slightly haughty expression. She's just as impressive now, except she was softer then, somehow. I hope that when I'm older I don't look back and think I was nicer, before. When I was looking at her papers I heard a noise down below. Aunt Lily got out of a strange car, an old black Peugeot driven by a black man. A European got out too. I stuffed the papers back in her desk and ran down the stairs. She could tell at once I'd done something wrong. She went inside and left me talking to the stranger. Tall, very polite, and deeply mysterious. His name is David. To fill the silence between us I invited him to Aunt Lily's party. What will she think of me?

I remember clearly what I had thought: acting on Gustave's orders she spied on me constantly and, in my absence, systematically ransacked my papers.

That morning, on my way to Fort de France, my car began to wheeze and then knock loudly, forcing me to pull up in the square at La Trinité where I was quickly surrounded by a crowd of sullen teenagers who shuffled their feet in derisive silence and drew threateningly close. Their blockade had only symbolic significance. Clouds of steam poured from the engine as proof of my impotence. No one answered when I enquired after the nearest garage. I had spoken in patois which was doubtless a mistake.

Then Léopold's black Peugeot roared round the corner and out of sight. Within moments it reappeared, reversing at speed. The teenagers scattered as it braked sharply beside me and the square returned to silence. Léopold, at the wheel, refused to acknowledge our long-standing acquaintance, likewise the girl Christophine who sat stiffly on the back seat looking in the opposite direction.

A tall, broad-shouldered man with a shock of thick fair hair climbed out of the Peugeot and offered his assistance. He spoke fluently but with a foreign, stilted accent. He managed to frown and smile at the same time, blessed with that peculiarly British habit of regarding the world as a puzzle constructed for the amusement of small children. We looked into the engine. The man pulled a few wires, poked knowledgeably at various bits of machinery and announced it was hopeless. His vocabulary was not catholic enough to explain what was wrong but it was clear that the problem defeated him. I thanked him for his kindness and shook his hand, which left a smudge of black oil on my palm.

'Taverner,' he announced abruptly, wiping his hands on his trousers, 'David Taverner. Will you be all right?' The teenagers had closed in again, and stood around us in a circle.

'Quite all right, thank you. I'll get a taxi.'

He looked around the square and remarked rather superfluously, 'The taxis, they've all gone.'

'I shouldn't have long to wait, thank you.'

He walked several paces towards the Peugeot then stopped. 'I don't like leaving you here.' He glanced at the teenagers. 'Can we give you a lift?'

'I think we're travelling in different directions.'

'Are you going far?'

'Not really. Five kilometres or so . . .'

He looked at his watch, hesitated, then said decisively that they would take me home. I accepted his offer and was ushered into the back of the Peugeot next to Christophine who pressed herself against the door. Léopold watched us through the mirror.

'Where to *chef*?'

I gave Taverner the address of the plantation house, which Léopold knows as well as I do. We travelled a few minutes in uncomfortable silence, Christophine still huddled against the door as if I might contaminate her. Out of politeness I said to the young man, 'You don't appear to be French. May I ask where you're from?'

'England,' he said diffidently, 'though I was born in Palestine. Jerusalem, in fact. I'm working here. I write, you see.' It was, I believe, the only time he volunteered any information about himself.

'A writer. How interesting. I didn't catch your name?'

'Taverner. David Taverner. You won't have heard of me. I wouldn't call myself a writer, exactly.'

'But you *do* write?'

'Oh yes. Articles. Features. That kind of thing. I'm a journalist.'

'I tell Mr Taverner,' said Léopold, slapping the steering wheel as he drove and glancing in the mirror at Christophine, 'that if he writes the truth about us he'll end up writing poems, like Monsieur Césaire.'

'Mr Caesar?' asked Taverner, puzzled.

Léopold feigned surprise. 'You never heard of Mr Caesar? Hell of a guy, Mr Caesar. Said we would never invent anything. That we were just shoeshine boys and sorcerers. You should read him, *chef*. You can learn a lot from Mr Caesar.'

'I'm afraid my newspaper doesn't print poetry,' the Englishman observed cautiously.

'No *chef. Mauvais nègs*, that's all we are. Bad niggers. No poems but plenty of match reports. Same as here. English ones too . . . Good team, Arsenal United,' he muttered savagely. 'What do you think Christophine?'

'I think he's laughing at you,' she said, staring straight ahead.

We drove the rest of the way in silence, Léopold grinning to himself like a madman and Taverner playing his piano with large knuckled hands and smiling at me sheepishly over his shoulder from the front seat. I was heartily relieved when we drove through the iron gates to the plantation.

David Taverner helped me out of the car. By then he had smeared half the oil from my engine down his trouser legs. At that moment my niece came flying down the stairs, talking even more breathlessly than usual and flinging her arms around my neck as if she had not seen me in weeks. After introducing the young people I went inside to telephone the garage which took an inordinate length of time: the young illiterate at the other end of the line required a full description of my car (everyone knows the silver-grey Citroën) and the exact spot in the square where it was parked. To my surprise, when I returned the young man was still talking to Agnès. Léopold caught my eye and shrugged. Agnès broke off when she saw me and said that she had invited David (I am certain she used his Christian name, even then) to join us the following evening at a soirée I had arranged in honour of Claude whom I wished to introduce to the leaders of our small community. I tried to dissuade her.

'But he'd love to come. He's said so. That's right, isn't it David?' She touched his hand. He smiled weakly.

And turning to me, 'You see, Aunt Lily, it's all arranged.'

I felt unnaturally cross that she should thwart my intentions.

'In that case,' I remarked coldly, 'you hardly need my permission.'

Agnès hugged me and said, 'I knew you would understand.'

I left them alone and to this day do not know if the Englishman was as trapped into accepting the invitation as I was into giving it. From the house I heard Léopold's engine roar into action as he executed a maniacal three-point turn, the tyres slithering across the gravel, before he shot down the drive like a man possessed.

4

DAVID TAVERNER arrived at my party for Claude and was greeted by Agnès like a long-lost cousin. She kissed him warmly on the cheeks and clung to his arm as she leant negligently against him, whispering in his ear and making him laugh at private observations before she wilfully abandoned him – to Madame Ségovie, of all people, who had spent the evening fluttering her eyelashes at Claude across the room. She looked Taverner up and down and, clearly deciding he was of little consequence, started talking about her husband, the Secretary-General. I heard her say he was a 'good man' and 'particularly kind to animals'.

'I wouldn't doubt it for a moment, Madame.'

'You know they used to eat parrots here, the émigrés?' As she spoke she adjusted her green and white frock, an unwise choice for a woman of her circumference.

'I had no idea,' said Taverner, clearly out of his depth.

'Especially priests,' she went on emphatically. 'They made it quite a fashion.'

'Good heavens . . . How strange. It was a delicacy, perhaps?'

'You don't understand, Monsieur.' She stared firmly at a point between his eyes. 'The habit has in any case died out.'

'And the parrots too, no doubt,' said Taverner.

He was rewarded by one of the black looks to which we have become accustomed at the meetings of our committee on cultural affairs (a well-meaning if ineffectual body; we lack culture as much as we lack history but we must do our best). By the time Claude joined them, the pair stood back to back, having exhausted all possible subjects of common interest. Madame Ségovie gave my friend one of her more appealing smiles and turning to Taverner said grandly that the island was honoured by the presence of a great voice from the Americas, the voice of freedom and hope, a champion of the dispossessed. Tears glinted in her eyes as she spoke. To Claude she explained merely that David Taverner was a journalist of one sort or another, lodged at some disreputable hotel in Vauclin, the Hôtel des Innocents, of which she had never heard.

I smiled at the woman's peremptory manner and wished to join them myself but Eveline came to tell me she could not find the silver serving plates. She was suffering one of her bad spells and my presence was required at frequent intervals in the kitchen. On my return I noticed Emile Leclerc standing alone to one side of the room staring disdainfully over the heads of my guests. Leclerc, reputedly the island's leading historian, is curator of a small museum in Fort de France, a shabby affair full of stuffed animals, lost coins, faded love letters and inventories of slaves, all labelled methodically in Leclerc's near-illegible handwriting. He is a tall man and plays patience with Tarot cards.

Leclerc bowed when I joined him. At that moment Agnès slipped into the lamplight which outlined the contours of her breasts between her lace chemise. I saw it all. I saw Claude raise his glass. I saw Agnès pirouette coquettishly in the soft circle of light. I saw her smile as Taverner caught her eye. And I was suddenly afraid.

Emile Leclerc ignored my discomfort and launched immediately into his favourite topic of conversation: my stones, the ones that Agnès nicknamed the golliwog gods, which have belonged to my husband's family since the seventeenth century. Leclerc maintains one cannot personally own a piece of history and as the stones are undoubtedly the most important example of pre-Columbian mythology they belong rightfully in his museum and should not lie carelessly under the stars. I suspect more significantly he wishes to compose one of his labels for them. We have disputed ownership for so long that we know our arguments by heart. I have promised to bequeath him the stones in my will and until I die they will remain in my possession. André gave them to me and, besides, I have little patience with extinct mythologies.

'The stones,' he said, inspecting the wallpaper beyond my head, 'were not your husband's to give.'

'Come, come, Monsieur, you must do better than that.'

'They are part of our heritage.'

'And they are part of my life.'

'With respect, Madame, we don't go on for ever,' he replied with an air of fatuous conceit. Unable to think why I had invited him I left him staring at the wall – dreaming no doubt of history – and circulated among my guests, reassured by their familiar conversations. D'Aurigny, my closest neighbour, enumerated the dangers of *dissidence* (he considers even de Gaulle a dissident). Suzanne, his rather charming wife, talked to Geneviève Chaumeton about a salon specialising in gowns for ladies of a certain age. From several quarters I heard the latest scandal in the *métropole* which held out, we agreed, little hope for the future. Madame Delarue said she would eat lobster more frequently but could not bear to hear their screams.

Eveline's uncle whispered in my ear that I was required once more in the kitchen. His name is Georges Santos though he is known by everyone as Pépé. He doubles as my gardener – part-time – and that evening was dressed in a white, batman's jacket, several sizes too small, and black, pressed trousers that flapped above his ankles. Eveline adores him and I hire him largely on her account as he is precious little use to me. This time she had problems locating spare glasses which I found in a cupboard above the sink, where they always are. She swore she had looked there already. I returned to my guests.

Geneviève Chaumeton made space for me as I tried to pass her. 'We were just talking about your niece,' she said gushingly. 'Such a pretty girl, and so like your late husband's sister. Tall too, and those eyes. You must have noticed it, Alicia. What was she called – the middle sister?' She turned to her companion for inspiration. Suzanne d'Aurigny flushed with embarrassment and stuttered, 'I c-c-can't remember.'

I followed Geneviève's glance. Out on the veranda Agnès stood at the centre of a small group comprising Claude, my friend Achille Gonstran, the mayor of St Antoine, David Taverner, and, hovering in the background, Olivier d'Aurigny who had taken Agnès to Josephine's museum at Trois Ilets. Agnès looked, if truth were told, as if she flirted with all the men at once, not forgetting young d'Aurigny behind her. I trust it was unconscious on her part. She would catch one of them in her sights, pout prettily then devastate him with her most wayward smile so that even the mayor was subverted by her charm. At Agnès's side, David Taverner appeared to be staring down her chemise, a pretty piece of embroidered cotton and lace she had bought for a song in Fort de France and wore on every possible occasion because it showed her figure to the best advantage. When Pierre d'Aurigny approached us and began again on the subject of dissidence, I escaped to the veranda.

Agnès was talking animatedly – the heads of the men inclined towards her. She stopped mid-sentence at the sight of me.

'What were you saying, my dear?' I asked.

'Nothing, aunt, we were just talking.'

'About what?'

Claude, Gonstran and Taverner stared at my niece; Olivier d'Aurigny sidled away, sensing my hostility. Agnès tossed her head and pulled back the hair from her face. Then she practised her smile on me.

'Actually we were talking about . . . well, you . . .' she said, faltering as her courage failed her.

'Agnès was telling us about her father,' said Claude, coming to the girl's rescue, 'and how he wishes you to return to France.'

'I don't care to have my affairs broached in public.'

Claude said, 'We are, you must admit, among friends.' My expression told him that I admitted nothing.

'You know my views on the subject,' volunteered Gonstran.

'Don't be cross, Aunt Lily,' said Agnès, taking David Taverner by the elbow. He seemed surprised by such an open gesture of affection and held his arm in front of his body, awkwardly, with Agnès clinging to it like a raft. She laughed and said excitedly, 'Mayor Gonstran's been telling the most wonderful stories . . . The mynah bird. Tell Aunt Lily the story of the mynah bird.'

'Oh, it's not so funny,' mumbled Gonstran with increasing distress.

'Go on. For my sake.' Gonstran shook his head. Agnès turned to me and said in a rush, 'There was this man, you see. He bought a mynah bird in the market. They're terribly rare, or something. Cost him a fortune. Then one morning the man shot himself. Through the head. Left a note saying he couldn't bear to hear the bird echo his laughter. Isn't that wonderful?'

'It's true,' said Gonstran very quietly. 'It happened to a friend of mine.'

Agnès could not have heard him. Her laughter rang out into the night. Perhaps it is only the young who do not fear the mocking echo of their own amusement.

Achille Gonstran turned away and stood to one side of the company where he was joined by David Taverner who had extricated himself from Agnès's embrace. Although I was not party to their conversation I understand the mayor was most concerned that Taverner should not write about the flowers.

'Flowers?' asked Taverner. 'What flowers?'

'Frangipani . . . Oleander . . . You know what I mean. Tropical flowers. Like your daffodils.'

'I'm not a botanist, for God's sake.'

'I never said you were.'

'Then why should I . . .'

'Too damned exotic,' said Gonstran vehemently. 'It's like a disease. If you don't want to catch it take my advice and keep off the flowers.'

Poor Taverner. People were always dictating to him what he should write. *If you write the truth about us you will end up writing poems, like Mr Caesar*. They offered him explanations, and helpful advice, and he never quite followed what anyone was trying to tell him.

I stood with Claude on the edge of the veranda listening to the chattering of my guests drift gently into the thick warm night to join the persistent chorus of cicadas and the throaty call of bullfrogs. It was all so civilised and I remembered those other evenings when André and I had entertained our friends – we were renowned throughout Martinique for our hospitality. Claude felt exactly as I did; I knew that from his quiet manner and our hands which touched lightly on the rails. We had no need of words.

Eveline was tugging at my elbow. As I followed her inside Madame Ségovie saw Claude alone and pounced, that is the only word for it, hectoring him at once with her views on Literature. She is a large woman, not easily gainsaid.

In the kitchen I found Pépé with his feet on the table and remarked that I had hired the man to look after my guests, not to lounge about on my furniture. He shambled into a corner and busied himself with a fresh tray of drinks, muttering under his breath and throwing me resentful glances out of the corner of his eye. I warned Eveline she must watch the man more carefully if he were to continue in my employment.

Then a scream rang out like a cat screeching in the night. Pépé stumbled with the tray of drinks and rolled his eyes wildly around their sockets. My heart froze. Eveline fell to her knees among broken glassware, crossing herself furiously. I rushed back along the corridor to the sitting-room where my guests cowered against one wall. Agnès was standing near the window, blood dripping from a cut on her forehead, red blood, bright red, shocking. I noticed that Leclerc was missing.

Agnès was close to collapse. Claude moved swiftly and taking her in his arms led her to an armchair. She staggered as he held her close. He put her down but she clung to him, forcing him to perch awkwardly on the armrest, holding her head against his chest. An ugly red stain grew on his shirt.

The guests inched nervously away from the wall. They started talking at once, a fearful babble of voices. Eveline and her uncle crept into the room, holding each other tightly by the hand. The man's eyeballs continued to roll skywards. Eveline broke into a litany about assorted spirits, mysteries, *les anges*. I quickly silenced her. There are no angels here.

'A stone,' someone called shrilly, 'through the window.' 'No, that window,' said another. A third said, 'Over there!' Madame Ségovie was adamant that stones were flung through several windows at once. Mayor Gonstran strode to the open door. 'Is anyone there?' he called. Silence. Only the insects replied. He paused, sniffed the air, then marched firmly down the steps, calling to our invisible assailant. His voice grew fainter as he hurried off into the plantation.

I turned towards my niece. Claude smoothed her hair, matted with blood above the cut. He spoke to her gently, soothingly, I could not catch his words. Taverner stood next to them, having pushed his way through the small crowd gathered round her, and offered Claude his handkerchief, the one stained with oil. Claude brushed it aside. The Englishman looked hurt and thrust his hands in his pockets. Pierre d'Aurigny still argued loudly about the stone's exact trajectory.

Agnès stared up at Claude. He smiled and stroked her face. They looked quite separate from the rest of us. My heart constricted at another memory, when Angeline had fallen by the river into André's arms, my husband and her brother. She cut her head on the rocks and smeared her face with blood. André held her, as Claude did Agnès, and drove my happiness away. Claude saw me looking at them and said I must not worry, the wound would heal. Agnès smiled faintly. I fetched her brandy and held the glass to her lips because her hands shook. She looked a child again. Taverner asked if he might help. Taking pity on him I suggested he went in search of Gonstran. Relieved at having some occupation he set off at once.

The other guests looked at each other circumspectly, their nervous chatter exhausted. The women fingered their jewels while the men downed drinks which Pépé offered around the room, glasses rattling on his tray. Eveline stood in a corner where she talked to herself, hands gripped in prayer.

The evening was in ruins. I called my guests together and said I would quite understand if they wanted to leave, which they did with unseemly haste – no one offering to stay in case of further attacks. I saw them off, ashamed by their faint-heartedness. Even Madame Ségovie seemed reduced in size. As she left she said that Señor Cerda was magnificent.

Claude had lain Agnès on the sofa, her lace chemise flecked with blood. She would not wear it again. Claude too was tainted. He sat by her side, holding one wrist as if to take her pulse and with the other hand wiped a trickle of blood from her neck. I felt numb.

A noise outside the house. We turned in unison as Gonstran ran up the steps, Taverner trailing some distance behind.

'What did you see?' I asked. 'Who did it?'

Gonstran shrugged, his eyes glistening in the light. They had seen nothing, heard nothing, found no footmarks, clues, no trace of our attackers, nothing to explain or justify what had happened.

'It's always the same in Martinique,' said Gonstran wearily, 'no one is *ever* responsible.'

The stoning of Agnès was reported two days later in the newspapers. A leading article in *France-Antilles* suggested that such random attacks – even if the girl had escaped with a few stitches and a large bruise on her forehead – could seriously damage the island's economy. Without a tourist industry the island would die. And tourists did not care to be stoned. The editor called for the immediate incarceration of the culprits to demonstrate that a disregard for the law did not pay, in the end.

As the mayor predicted, no one claimed responsibility. Secretly I suspected Eveline's daughter, Yvette, to whom Agnès had given a doll, a very expensive doll dressed in gingham with fat pink cheeks, fair curls, and real tears that flowed when you pressed a button. Soon after the gift had been ungraciously received the doll was discovered near the hurricane shelter, decapitated. The most we could elicit was that the doll had met with 'an accident'.

Agnès herself quickly recovered and regarded the whole episode as an adventure. She was thrust temporarily into the limelight, even in Europe as Taverner had wired the story home to his newspaper. I reminded her that she had been hit by chance and any one of us could have suffered the same fate. A couple of scandal sheets appeared which criticised Achille Gonstran for attending social functions hosted by *les gens de la métropole*. Claude and Olivier arrived with flowers for Agnès. I wrote to my brother requesting he recall the girl to France. Gustave replied she would leave with me. We had reached an impasse and all of us misread the signs.

5

SEVERAL DAYS after this unhappy event, when our lives had returned to normal, I drove Claude into Fort de France for a meeting of the Cultural Committee, at Madame Ségovie's request. As I knew he would have little interest in composing letters to the President of the Republic I said we would arrive at midday when the main business was over. We parked across the street from the Schoelcher library, a ridiculously ornate building more reminiscent of the British Raj than the French West Indies. (I think it significant that the British should devastate so completely a nation's taste.) The crowds were thicker than usual and we had to fight our way through a noisy confusion of taxi drivers, hired cars, motorcyclists and hawkers selling straw hats and Josephine key-rings to the tourists.

Inside, the library rustled with whispered conversations. As we climbed the stairs I pointed out André's collection of books which I had donated after his death and received in return an invitation to join the Committee, to which I have belonged ever since in a supernumerary capacity. Madame Ségovie stood up as we entered the room and welcomed Claude effusively. The shutters were drawn against the sunlight and the room was stiflingly hot. Around a table in the centre sat a sprinkling of the more regular attenders who regarded Claude, our prize exhibit, with ill-concealed curiosity. Madame Ségovie hovered about our elbows, apologising for the poor attendance which she attributed to the *lycée* contingent who had walked out *en masse* a few minutes earlier in protest at the Committee's decision to fund the translation of Molière and Racine into Creole, a further example, they felt, of French neo-imperialism. Sartre and Lévi-Strauss were, I believe, their favoured authors. As they walk out of most meetings they can hardly be considered members at all. Claude made some consoling remarks and with a flourish shook each one present by the hand, giving the impression that it was he who was honoured by the introduction. Madame Ségovie made space for him at the head of the table and I was forced to take a seat near the bottom between Emile Leclerc and young Boukman who edits a literary review read mostly by his friends.

Had I not retained my copy of the minutes I would recall barely a word that was spoken. Though useful as an *aide-mémoire*, they give nothing of the flavour of that interminable discussion. Leclerc, eyes shut, entwined his legs around the furniture. I wondered if he had fallen asleep. Boukman nibbled at his lips and looked ready to take refuge under the table while Margoulis, as always, exuded his peculiar brand of self-satisfaction. A novelist who has not written a word of note in twenty years, he looks like a shoeshine boy but for his coarse white hair. It is rumoured he has never left the island because he cannot bear to explain who he is. My contribution was as usual omitted from the record. I said we were in danger of turning Claude into a circus trick and ourselves into a jamboree.

Item 6

Mme Ségovie, on behalf of the Committee, welcomed M. Claude Cerda from Santiago, Chile. As chairwoman of the Action Committee she was honoured to invite him to a soirée at which, before a specially invited audience, he might read from his latest works. She added that as the Committee had agreed to defray most of his expenses during his stay on the island it was only proper that the people of Martinique should reap some benefit. *M. Cerda* thanked the chairwoman for her kind words of welcome but said that when he had accepted the Committee's original offer he had not realised that it carried certain obligations. He most emphatically could not write to order and his progress was only moderate as he was attempting to break new ground. *Mme Ségovie* said he had surely written something of merit in the months he had been here. *M. Lafayette* explained that the Committee was financed by the Department of Fine Arts and Culture who expected it to take the lead in putting Martinique on the cultural map. *M. Cerda* pointed out that he was not a cartographer. He raised a further problem, namely that he had encountered few people on the island who were fluent enough in Spanish to understand a word he said. *Mme Ségovie* suggested that poetry was a universal language and that even if his audience could not understand, they could appreciate the cadence of his sentences. Spanish, she felt, was a very musical language, a subject on which M. Cerda could express no opinion as Spanish was his mother tongue.

The proposal was thrown open to discussion and it was noted that the preparation of translations could overcome M. Cerda's objections. *M. Cerda* maintained that he did not write in French. *M. Margoulis* offered the assistance of members of the Committee who were not, he said, untalented in these matters. A novel of his own had been expected to win the Prix Goncourt in 1968 and a poem he had written on the subject of electricity pylons had been included in the *baccalauréat* syllabus for 1964–5 and taught throughout French dominions. *M. Cerda* declined this offer on the grounds that he did not write poems by committee either.

M. Boukman questioned M. Cerda about his current themes as he edited a small review, *Chanson Antillaise*, which would be honoured to print some of his more recent works. *M. Cerda* said he was writing about love. *M. Boukman* regretted that this might raise some ideological difficulties following a recent decision of his editorial board to ban any mention of love which they condemned as a counter-revolutionary cult of the personal. *M. Cerda* said he had never been considered in such a light before and suggested with the greatest respect that the members of the board did not know what they were talking about. *M. Leclerc* enquired whether M. Cerda's poems had been written from an historical perspective. *M. Cerda* said he did not understand the question but offered for M. Boukman's consideration a series of poems about the house he had built on the coast near Valparaíso, Chile, to which he intended to retire with his daughters. *M. Boukman* queried whether writing about houses was not more counter-revolutionary than writing about love. In the ensuing debate *M. Cerda* relied on the authority of Gaston Bachelard who said it was important not to confuse one's attic with one's cellar. However, the said Bachelard had also written that it was impossible to imagine an empty wardrobe, which considerably weakened his argument. *Mme Ségovie* asked how a discussion of furniture was relevant to the matter in hand.

M. Lavallée suggested that the Committee should consider the translation of M. Cerda's work into Creole, a sufficiently radical gesture to overcome any possible doubts about its political suitability. *Mme Ségovie* pointed out that the Committee had already allocated its funds under the Creole budget and the Committee's constitution did not contain a mechanism for overturning decisions already taken. *M. Lavallée* proposed that the meeting should start again from the beginning and moved that the minutes up to this point should be erased. It was noted, however, that the absence of Messieurs Sainte-Rose, Gosier, Duval and Tributin from the *lycée* rendered this course of action impossible. *M. Lavallée* wished it to be recorded that he was profoundly dissatisfied with Committee procedures and *it was agreed* that a subcommittee should be established to review the situation. M. Lavallée was offered and accepted the chair.

Returning to the subject of M. Cerda's poetry reading, *Mme Ségovie* summed up the advantages and disadvantages of her original proposal, modified to include the translation of selected poems into French, a matter to which M. Cerda agreed to devote some attention. It was further suggested that the meeting should be thrown open to the public. A vote was taken and only Mme de Ste Croix dissented. *The motion was therefore carried* and a subcommittee, chaired by Mme Ségovie, established to hire suitable premises and organise refreshments. *M. Margoulis* suggested that M. Achille Gonstran, Mayor of St Antoine, be invited in his official capacity to give a speech of welcome. A provisional date of 1 May was *agreed*, subject to the aforesaid arrangements proving satisfactory. As there was no other business, the meeting closed at approximately 1.30 p.m.

When the meeting broke up Claude skilfully warded off an invitation to lunch with our chairwoman and was then joined by Margoulis, the former novelist, and Boukman who engaged my friend in renewed discussion of his themes. (They had neither, I trust, noticed the look Claude gave me when he said he wrote of love.) Boukman still hoped to snatch some literary crumbs for his magazine and Margoulis simply wanted to impress. Madame Ségovie, clutching a batch of papers to her ample bosom, stood on the sidelines. As the men parted Margoulis said he looked forward to hearing the work of a fellow artist, even poems about wardrobes. Claude laughed and told me later the man had a fine sense of humour.

At the library counter below Claude shook the hand of each pretty girl, blowing them kisses as he swept outside like a presidential candidate while Mme Ségovie, Boukman and I followed more meekly at his heels.

On the journey home Claude asked me why I had voted against the motion that he should give a public reading of his works. I invented some reply and omitted to say that having heard some of his poems already I considered them my own. We drove in companionable silence until we passed into a rainstorm and the strength of the deluge forced me to halt by the roadside. With the windows shut and the thundering of rain on metal I felt cocooned in another world, just the two of us, and very much at peace. Then Claude asked me what I knew about Agnès and David Taverner.

The girl often featured in our conversations. It was as if Claude had lost touch with the young – his daughters lived in Vienna with their mother – and Agnès opened up again that magic kingdom full of puffed-up dreams and elusive hopes. (I, on the other hand, am happy to be older, now.) He asked me all manner of questions, about her short-lived and haphazard education among the Sisters of the Sacred Heart, the nature of her friendships, her feelings towards Gustave and Marie-Louise, her most intimate of thoughts. I could not answer one half of them and was often forced to question her myself to provide my friend the necessary information.

As for Agnès and the Englishman, I said that they were friends in the way young people are. Claude disagreed. The previous day he had observed a meeting between the two of them on the Savannah, by the statue of Josephine. Taverner had arrived first. He read a book, looked at his watch, walked several times around the statue, pausing each time to read the inscription. At the same time an islander, who wore a black beret and limped conspicuously, walked around the statue in the opposite direction before strolling off to the seafront where he sat on the wall and rolled himself a cigarette. Then Agnès came. The two embraced and spoke hurriedly before leaving in opposite directions.

I was frankly bemused by this information. Everyone meets by the statue of Josephine. We listened to the rain beating about our heads, and I noticed Claude gripping his seat. I wondered what troubled him. The meeting seemed harmless enough.

'That's not all,' he said emphatically, disappointed by my lack of response. 'Before parting the Englishman gave Agnès a parcel which she hid in her bag, first checking that no one was looking.'

'A large parcel?' Claude gestured with his hands. Not large, obviously, and shaped like a fish.

'I really think . . .'

'You should look after her better,' he said, turning towards me with a strange look on his face, pained and almost angry. 'You must talk to the girl and find out what's going on between them.'

'I don't see what's upset you. Why not ask her yourself?'

'The girl is none of my business. You're her guardian.'

'We shall see,' I replied quietly, 'we shall see.'

This exchange was the closest we ever got to a quarrel. As the rain had slackened we resumed our journey and when I returned home, intending to speak to Agnès as Claude wished, the girl was out. I went straight to her room where, on the table by the window, I found her diary and a bundle of letters. The clasp on the diary was locked so I put it aside and read a letter from her friend Simone, ignoring several from Marie-Louise, Agnès's mother, knowing her style well enough to be certain that her letters would reveal nothing of significance. Simone's correspondence yielded little, however. She talked incessantly of young men from a certain cavalry regiment and particularly one called Louis Gavron who seemed a special favourite of Agnès. The rest of the letter was composed of gossip and a distressing account of a quarrel with her father – she seemed a most unsuitable acquaintance. When Agnès came back, her face burnt by the wind and her hair now bleached almost white, I quite forgot to ask her about Taverner, and the strange parcel she had hidden in her bag.

Claude did not refer to the episode again and it quickly slipped my mind. I continued to visit him in the afternoons after his work was done, and was relieved that he questioned me less about Agnès. We returned to our old conversations which I had loved more than anything in the world. Sometimes he would recite poems which I did not understand, of course, knowing no word of Spanish, but their rhythms were simply the most beautiful I had ever heard. He told me more about his twin daughters, Isabella and Rosa, and described for me the house he had built on a rocky stretch of coast near Valparaíso, a lonely place devoid of trees or any human habitation. For Isabella, his favourite, he had built a bare empty space at the back overlooking the wastelands. Rosa's room, on the other hand, had a view of the ocean so that she could count the waves and watch the sunsets.

In return I introduced André. My own ancestors are scattered throughout the old colonies, all explorers of one kind or another, which explains why André was attracted to me on one of his infrequent visits to Europe. We met at a reception arranged by some learned society to commemorate Great Aunt Mathilde's disappearance in the jungles of Brazil and André sat next to me at dinner. He had recently been awarded a special prize for a treatise on Ptolemy. I found him exceedingly handsome with his weather-beaten face, and neat, very black moustache. Throughout the meal he entertained me with exquisite stories and I laughed gaily as much at his accent as his tales. Unable to pronounce the letter 'r', he nevertheless said 'twès bon, twès bon' at every opportunity, a speech defect, I thought, until I came here and found that everyone speaks like that. I do it myself sometimes, much to Agnès's amusement.

My mother was reluctant to agree to our marriage, believing I could have made a better match and stayed in Europe closer to her side. But she made enquiries which proved satisfactory, if not brilliant, and after our wedding day we set sail for Martinique. I never once regretted my decision. André was a good-hearted man whom I dearly loved. Though he rarely left the island he collected encyclopedias and sent away to France for manuals of exploration which taught him how to navigate by stars. This same collection is now housed in the Schoelcher library except for his maps and one or two instruments which have rusted abominably in this hateful climate. All this I told Claude as we sat on his balcony or walked along the black volcanic sands.

Then one day, a little over a week after the stoning, Claude looked up from his chair and said – apropos of nothing – 'Which room will *you* have?'

'Which room? What do you mean?'

'In my house. I'll build you a room. Your very own room. You can have a whole wing if you like.'

'But Claude . . .'

He leapt from his seat and stood looking out at the evanescent lights on the water. I could not see his face. I suppose all our conversations had led to this and though I should have been prepared I found myself lost for words.

Claude turned towards me, catching the gilded sun on his furrowed, peasant face.

'I'm not sure,' I said. 'I really can't answer . . .'

'A wing or a room?'

'Not a wing. That's too much.'

'What then?' he insisted. The lights sparking off the water haloed his face like a hero's. He would not be denied.

I shut my eyes and imagined the house on the cliff tops and the rocky wilderness beyond. 'Not a wing,' I said, 'just a little room at the centre of your house. To feel the others around me.'

When I dared to look at him again his gentle smile told me I had answered aright. He sat beside me, and offered to take some space from Isabella. I warned that I must never displace his daughters.

'She'll gladly sacrifice the room. She has acres already. You'll love them, my little girls.'

'How do you know?'

'I do.'

'They may be jealous.'

He looked surprised. 'They have no cause for that.'

'Jealous of my little room.'

'Nonsense. I'll send for them at once.'

His haste infected me. He wanted me to meet them immediately, and without further ceremony he told me of their mother, of the hats she wore, and her outlandish behaviour, and of his other lovers, a girl with violet eyes, daughter of a General, the woman he had cherished in Batavia, a Russian dancer . . . It seemed an odd conversation to follow so quickly a proposal of marriage.

'My dear Alicia,' he said warmly, 'we'll get on famously. Like houses.'

We fell silent as I considered his offer, knowing no woman on earth could resist, but wondering what André might think of my forsaking him.

The next day I steeled myself to call at the cemetery. The sun was at its highest and the graves blinded me with their whiteness. It was the first time in fifteen years that I had brought no flowers, so I borrowed a rose from a nearby grave and laid it on André's resting place. We sat for a time, very peacefully, then I told him of all the other offers of marriage I had received since he left me, which I had never thought to mention. Claude was different, however. He would surely approve: Claude had done things, met people, travelled several times around the world. He was a poet, I said proudly, a good one, and held a string of honorary degrees from major universities. I felt certain that André gave me his blessing.

Weeds grew up around his grave. I made a note to speak to Father Thomas who should supervise his staff more closely if they were not to take advantage of him.

At dinner that night I told Agnès about my change in

plans. She wanted to write immediately to Gustave for if I were to marry Claude my return to France was out of the question. I said I was not ready to inform her father and the rest of the pack, and made her promise she would speak of this to no one. We drank champagne and though the girl looked surprised at my news she quickly warmed to the notion and drank repeated toasts to our happiness, with the result that she retired to bed a little unsteadily and bumped into the furniture. She was a good girl, I thought, whom I had badly misjudged.

In the days that followed my poet welcomed me in his house. He did not refer again to his question of rooms but our relationship had subtly altered as we shared a future as well as our pasts. Once, in the time normally reserved for his work, I caught sight of him from the headland striding along the beach, head down, hands behind his back. Agnès walked at his side. I smiled at the sight: from a distance one could mistake her for his daughter.

6

2 April

AUNT LILY'S party, much as Maman's except the guests wore fancy dress and half the faces were black. David came. I feel very attracted to him though he's not exactly good-looking. On the surface he's friendly and open but you know you're not getting through. It's just part of his defences. His dress sense is terrible. He wore a dirty old jacket, a kind of muddy beige, that fell off his shoulders with a rip up the back he'd mended with staples. I think he wore desert boots. But he has nice hands – very solid and strong. He said he was a foreign correspondent though he seems a little accident prone. At Christmas they sent him to Jordan with instructions to track down a Welshman called Jones, suspected of trading guns with the Bedouins. He found him in a resthouse during a power failure and the two became friends. Then word got round that there were two troublemakers at large and David was brought back at once, in disgrace. There was also some doubt about whether he had found the right Jones. I tried not to laugh because he looked so solemn and obviously takes it to heart.

Was introduced to the mayor, who's black and looks very kind. He told stories then wished he hadn't. To hunt the manicou – a large black rat with startled eyes – you freeze the poor creature in the headlights of your car then whack it on the head with a club. I took this for a joke until Claude whispered he was talking of colonialism.

The house like a ship in the night and then I was hit by a stone thrown through the window. It caused quite an uproar – most of the women were screaming – and everyone scuttled away as soon as they knew I was all right. The cars were brought to the front door and no one walked down the drive in case the people who attacked me should be hiding in the bushes. Aunt Lily sent for the doctor and made it plain she considered it all my fault.

3 April

Claude and Olivier brought me flowers and I have a large brown and yellow bruise on my forehead, enormous, held together by black stitches which look like insects. Outside my window Claude talked to Aunt Lily. They thought I was asleep. He asked how long I would stay. My aunt seems to think my visit is almost over. He made some comment about how I was like a very bright star that burns itself out several million light years before the others. She seemed to know what he meant. Perhaps Uncle André taught her astronomy.

Then David called to interview me for his paper. This caused a number of problems because the doctor had told me to stay in bed and Aunt Lily didn't think it right for him to talk to me in my room. We compromised in the end by leaving the door open. David sat at the end of the bed, very intent, writing down everything I said in a notebook. It was all very businesslike and slightly unnerving. He watches me with deep brown eyes. I look away, forget about him, then when I return to his face he's still observing me, taking notes, remembering. I wonder what he makes of me.

4 April

If they show me a stone, I'll say stone and they'll say stone. If they show me a tree, I'll say tree and they'll say tree. If they show me blood I'll say blood and they'll say PAINT.

5 April

David called with a cutting from his newspaper. I made five lines in the foreign news. I was disappointed – he asked so many questions – but he said his story was cut. We went south to Sainte Anne where he met a group of men called the *Santanistes* (I thought at first he meant devils). I had to wait for him in the car under the trees, although I wanted to go with him. It seems the *Santanistes* wouldn't like it. He was away for ages so I walked along the fine white sands, the surface of the water as still as glass, no wind, no surf, only the burning sun and a mirage in my head. D. was thoughtful on his return and said little for the rest of the day. We went round the coast, got caught in a rainstorm, kissed under a tree. I feel safe in his arms although Aunt Lily doesn't really approve and Maman would think him a mess. He doesn't like Martinique. It's much too green, he says, and overflowing with water.

6 April

Angeline never married and never gave birth to a daughter. They checked for me in the Public Records Office because I was sure I'd made a mistake. She was the only Angeline de Ste Croix registered on the island who was born and died but that's all. Poor Angeline. Perhaps Eveline made it all up.

The business took longer than I had expected and David had almost given up hope. He looked very relieved to see me and though he wouldn't tell me what he's up to he believes he's being followed, that he keeps seeing the same faces in the crowds: a man with a squint and another, much more sinister, who wears dark glasses and a beret and is always smoking a cigarette out of the corner of his mouth. He tried to point someone out to me but there were so many people around that I couldn't work out who he meant. He asked me to do him a favour. (I'd do anything for him, if only he'd let me.) He asked me to look after his gun. I thought he was joking but he wasn't. He put both hands on my shoulders and said he knew I could be trusted. That he could turn to no one but me. I suggested that if he was that worried he should throw the gun away but he said it had belonged to his grandfather.

When he gave me the gun I noticed Claude sitting in the distance reading a newspaper. He didn't see us but we must be very careful. It struck me suddenly that David was a spy.

7 April

Last night I was woken by a terrible sound, like the cry of a child tormented in hell. I'm sure they suffer more than we do. I couldn't stand it. I had to know what it was. As soon as I opened my door the crying stopped, cut off instantly. Only an echo remained. Very slowly I walked down the corridor which shone in the moonlight. Fear has never touched me like this before. The moon threw slatted shadows across the floor and all Aunt Lily's objects seemed for a moment to be in the wrong place. Someone had switched them round. Uncle André and his sisters under the *fromager*, her blue glass vases, the silver candlesticks. All jumbled up and confused. Another cry. I ran back to bed and only slept with the dawn. Someone had walked the house and tried to give me a message. This morning everything was back in its proper place. My aunt swears she heard nothing and Eveline was at her uncle's so I'll never know who called to me in the night.

Eveline says that if I light a candle the spirits will be frightened away, and that the insects that fly about the lamps aren't insects at all but something else: dead souls that haven't reached a state of grace.

Olivier came for lunch. As Aunt Lily was away in Fort de France at some meeting or other the house was ours. I took him into my room but nothing happened. He seemed terribly bashful and when he sat on the bed he pressed his knees together. We then went swimming with some friends of his, two brothers and a girl called Hélène. They played games in the sand and were disappointed I wouldn't join in. I thought they were showing off. On the way home the boys told me of a cock fight they'd seen. One of the birds was nearly pecked to death. It lay in the dirt, covered in blood and bald patches, twitching. The owner picked it up, put its head in his mouth, and sucked. It made me feel sick. The others joked about Olivier and me. About my bruises and how he must have hit me. Olivier turned scarlet and I pretended not to hear. When I got home Aunt Lily looked rather odd. She kept staring at me surreptitiously and asked all sorts of questions about Simone. She's never shown much interest before.

8 April

Met Claude in the café. He was on wonderful form though he hadn't slept at all because he had a weird visitor in the middle of the night. A man called Hector with curly black hair, a lop-sided grin that revealed a missing front tooth, and wild claims to be a 'wanted man'. Claude said he was probably a lunatic. He and his friends had blown up a school and organised an ambush for the Préfet, only the man changed his route and they netted a bunch of American tourists instead who didn't realise their guns were real.

Claude couldn't sit still. He kept leaping up to show me how Hector had appeared in the moonlight, crazy eyes and dramatic waving around of his arms. Hector had broken down the door then sat on Claude's bed as if nothing had happened. He had a problem, he said, a terrible problem, so terrible he had come down from the hills under cover of darkness to seek Claude's advice. But he wouldn't get to the point; seemed much more anxious to talk about literature. He said they'd all heard of Claude and admired his work. His own favourite was a poem about machine-guns in the desert and he was most put out when Claude explained it was a metaphor for love. He changed his mind on the spot, declaring he preferred the one on the ramparts when the world blows up. All the time Claude was trying to prod him into revealing his problem. Hector seemed embarrassed by the whole thing and no longer knew what to say. Finally, after enormous coaxing, he announced sheepishly he had a problem with history. Claude wanted to laugh but wasn't sure if the man was mad. 'He stalks through the night to talk to me of *history*?' By now Claude was striding about the café and everyone was watching us, hugely amused. The real problem, it seems, was that Hector felt he didn't have any history. Whatever he had belonged to other people. His ancestors had been brought over here and dropped in the shit. Now they couldn't get out of it, out of all the shit. It was as if there was a hole in their memories and they'd fallen in. And nothing happened. Claude reminded him of the volcano, and earthquakes, which Hector dismissed as Acts of God, not happenings at all. He was just a wrong-coloured Frenchman on the wrong side of the ocean. They'd colonised his head. To prove his point he rattled off the *Marseillaise*, word-perfect though horribly out of tune. I couldn't stop laughing when Claude sang it for me. The others in the café turned their backs on us. They didn't understand it was a joke.

Claude tried to help him. Said he knew just how he felt. They had a saying in Chile, *no pasa nada*, nothing happens. In the end they're right. Even revolutions can't change the world. Claude looked sad when he said this and suddenly shut up. Because of the other people I couldn't touch him. I asked what was wrong. He said that Hector reminded him of the Teoponte guerillas who had set off for the Bolivian jungle with their sandwiches, like children on a Sunday School outing. I expect he said so to this lunatic because the man became very offended and swore his group meant business. They owned a couple of machine-guns, French army issue, and a collection of knives and machetes. Claude asked if they wished to shoot down the moon. Hector drew himself up to his full height (he was very tall, Claude said, taller than David) and announced they needed guns to execute a kidnap. Then he protested they didn't want to hurt anyone. It was a gesture, nothing more. Claude said it was impossible to provoke social change without hurting someone in the process, there were always victims, and anyway, from what he heard he doubted if they could kidnap their grandmothers. The man loped off in the moonlight. I think there must have been something terribly brave about him.

After Claude told me about Hector he fell into one of his blacker moods. I tried to cheer him up but he suddenly jumped to his feet and went out – didn't even pay for the drinks. Left me wondering what was going on. This crazy visitor must have upset him. He had started to say the world had had enough of symbols, then he lost me. Or I lost him. He's the most extraordinary man I've ever met.

9 April
David called briefly on his way up north with Léopold and a very plain girl called Christophine who refused to shake my hand. She pretended she hadn't seen me though we were standing right next to each other. They only stayed a few minutes and I couldn't understand why they'd come. David kept his hands in his pockets and looked miserable. He's still being followed, he says, though not all the time. He hasn't found the story he's looking for and may have to leave soon. Perhaps he came to say goodbye. Aunt Lily watched us all the time from the veranda and I felt her eyes on my back. Afterwards I found Eveline alone in the kitchen gutting the fish for supper and we talked a bit about Angeline. Eveline didn't work here at the time and all she knows are the things people say. When I questioned her she wiped her hands on her apron, leaving smears of fish entrails, and said it was none of my business. Then she broke into patois and I turned to find Aunt Lily in the doorway. She spoke curtly to Eveline and said nothing at all to me.

10 April
Like David, I'm certain someone's following me. Someone larger than Yvette. A man. I think I know who it is but daren't tell my aunt or she'll send me home. I think she's

spying on me too. Everyone is. I try not to care. I want to write poems on the soles of your feet so that you may walk on beautiful words.

11 April

David's room, on the first floor, looks out to the Atlantic. Bare floorboards, an unmade bed, peeling paint, a table in front of the balcony on which stands his typewriter and papers held down by stones. We drew the shutters and I lay in his arms listening to the roar of the surf and the waves pounding on the beach. It's strange how large men can be so very gentle. I'm glad he hasn't gone home. I imagined he had picked me off the streets and taken me upstairs to kill the boredom of tropical afternoons. We lay there till it got dark and I like to think I'm not the first woman to have slept in his bed today. David says he spends much of his time by the window staring down at the street and the groups of fishermen who drink rum in the bar below and quarrel much of the night. I've reached the end of the road.

When I got home Aunt Lily was waiting for me. She was wearing her lilac dress again and jet black beads. She wanted me to dress for dinner and seemed pleased to have my company. When I was changed she told Eveline to bring some champagne and as soon as we had a glass in our hands she announced that Claude had asked her to marry him, and that they would move to his house on the coast, somewhere near Santiago. She looked ten years younger and very, very happy. I hope she didn't notice my surprise. Though they're obviously close I wouldn't have thought she was his kind of woman.

I didn't know what to say. At least she and I are on better terms than we've been for ages. After dinner she said she wished she'd kept Uncle André's piano because she wanted to hear me play. I didn't tell her I'd given it up. We sat talking outside and she told me very calmly about her plans, making me promise not to breathe a word to anyone as she didn't want gossip. She treated me like an equal and I wished it could always be like this. I began to understand about her and Claude, and we went to bed friends.

12 April

Louis wrote again, mostly about Simone. He says they meet almost every day to talk about me. She can have him for all I care, and his stupid promises. Aunt Lily was singing when I got up. She's wonderful and I love her more than ever. But as I had a hangover she was a little too bright and cheerful so I went out for a walk and found Claude striding along the beach. He looked unhappy and I didn't mention his marriage. In fact I said very little, just listened as he talked of Santiago and his friends who were rounded up after Allende and locked inside a football stadium where most of them were shot. When we reached the end of the beach he took me to a café, a shack really, where we drank beer out of bottles. Or rather I did. Claude turned his bottle round and round in his hands. He was very homesick and said he knew deep down he could never return to Chile. I asked what would happen to Aunt Lily, in that case, but he didn't seem to hear. Just muttered something about always being a vagabond, then stared out of the open window to the sea. I hope they know what they're doing. It's strange how I feel the need to protect her.

13 April

Dancing with David in a smoky basement off the rue Catherine in Fort de France. He holds me in his arms and we dance very closely to the music of Louisiana jazz played by a band of negroes with mean little smiles. He's not a very good dancer – bends his knees at the wrong places and trips over his feet as he tries to swirl me round. But he does his best. He runs his hand along the small of my back and pulls me to him so that I want him badly and know where this will end but do not hurry. I feel his breath on my neck, and the strength of his desire. Across the room a man with dark glasses smokes a cigarette, nonchalantly. He watches us above the heads of the other dancers, leering. I suspect that behind the glasses he has cruel eyes. As we're the only white people in the room I feel uneasy and tell David about the man with the glasses who by now has disappeared. David goes out to look for him so I sit down to wait. A man at the next table leans towards me and puts his hand on my knee. When I pull away he calls me a whore then changes his mind and declares I'm a *mal-cuit. On ne va pas te bouffer, les blancs*, he says under his breath. I follow David outside and find him talking to someone – a man. I'm not introduced. We drive quickly to Vauclin and lock ourselves in David's room where he takes me immediately, all the gentleness gone. As soon as he's finished he tells me to get dressed and drives me home without speaking a word. He doesn't even kiss me goodnight.

14 April

Aunt Lily showed me a box of old photographs, mostly of André and some of Sophie and Maryse. In one there's a face in the distance peering from behind the trees. I'm convinced it must be Angeline. Aunt Lily says she was frightened of growing old and after the age of twenty-five or so, refused to be photographed and never looked at herself in the mirror. I don't think that's possible, however. The face in the trees looked almost transparent. I showed it to Claude who suggested it was a trick of the light and not a face at all.

15 April

David continues his search for a story. On the Caravelle peninsula I saw him with a group of four or five men when he told me he was going to Case Pilote. The men sat on the ground looking rather dispirited while D. did most of the talking, as if he was giving a lecture. He leant against the wall of a rusty shed below the lighthouse, waving his arms around and looking quite angry. Or passionate. He's rarely like that with me. Every now and then the men would shake their heads and talk among themselves. Knowing I wouldn't be welcome I walked down by the mangrove where huge black crabs scuttled across the slime. I felt I crossed a moonscape. On my return the men had disappeared. They'd left their mark, however: a slogan slapped on the lighthouse with bright red paint, still wet, that warned of the coming of white niggers and black gods. Could David be worse than a spy?

7

DAVID TAVERNER was, as Agnès suspected, worse than a spy: he was a romantic. I should have warned the girl such men are the most dangerous of all. But would she have listened? She was headstrong, you see, and stubborn, a true daughter of my brother Gustave who continued to write each week seeking the date of our probable return. I replied by saying he could have Agnès back whenever he chose but he must bother me no more. This gave me a few moments peace.

My visits to Claude during this time were brief – no more than half an hour or so – as his work progressed slowly and he spent his days roaming the coastline in search of inspiration. For once I resented his work which withdrew him into a private world from which I was excluded. It was no better when I sat with him. He had become remarkably absent-minded and would repeat things he had said a few minutes earlier. I tried to draw him out, hurt by his manner which was somewhat cold, though that is a strange word to describe such a vigorous man.

As Agnès never accompanied me on my visits I was surprised that he agreed to dine with us on the night of her birthday, the 16th of April, when she had been with us for nearly five weeks. The only other guest she cared to invite was David Taverner, having dismissed Olivier d'Aurigny and his friends as 'children'.

That morning Agnès and I had driven over the hills to St Pierre which nestles on the leeward side of the volcano, a pretty town which reminded Agnès of the French Mississippi with its clapperboard houses, a tangle of power lines, and graceful balconies above the narrow streets. I showed her the Savannah of the White Fathers and the Savannah of the Black Fathers and we walked the stretch of main street towards the Rivière Roxelane. Agnès claimed to hear music playing, old Creole waltzes and *bel-airs*, and was blind to the hatred of the children who tagged at our heels, stopping when we stopped, staring when we stared, chattering to themselves like little devils. Agnès merely found them 'quaint'.

Claude arrived first when Agnès was still in her room. He had brought her a present, a collection of his early work with her name and the date inscribed inside. No message for the girl, of that I'm certain. He helped me arrange the table on the edge of the lawn, carrying out the glass candle-holders, the crystal glasses and bowls of sweet-smelling flowers, frangipani, wild roses, oleander. Then Taverner arrived, distressed to learn it was my niece's birthday as he had come empty-handed, and the three of us sat on the veranda waiting for Agnès.

A political rally was in progress down in the town from

which amplified phrases blew their way up the valley, truncated by sudden gusts of wind, phrases about freedom, motherlands and *gloire*. It was impossible to guess the speakers' political identity. Our orators employ a common stock of words which they invest with subtly altered shades of meaning. There are, for example, a number of possible interpretations of freedom.

Eveline announced that dinner was ready. Agnès called through the locked door that she would join us outside so I led Claude and David Taverner down the steps to the table under the trees where we took our seats and watched gentle shadows play across each other's faces. The Englishman remained silent most of the time, ill at ease. He played his imaginary piano in the air and gave me a headache.

Then Agnès appeared at the top of the steps. She wore a white lace dress that reached to the ground. I watched in anger as the girl stepped across the grass in white satin shoes, swirling wide skirts, her hair pulled back with long white ribbons. I could not bear the vision of her. David Taverner caught his breath as he stared at the cameo pendant hanging about her neck on a golden chain. Down the valley an invisible orator spoke of racial dreams.

When the girl reached the head of the table I stood up. 'Go inside at once and dress yourself properly.'

'What's wrong?' said Agnès, looking down at her white skirts. 'My dress is beautiful.'

'It's not *your* dress and no one gave you permission to wear it.'

Taverner pushed back his chair. 'It looks like a wedding dress,' he observed, still entranced by her neckline.

I glowered at him. 'I would be grateful, Monsieur, if you would leave this to me.'

'Aunt Lily, please. Just this once. It's my birthday after all.'

I felt a hand on my shoulder. It was Claude. 'Let her

alone, Alicia. Mademoiselle Montfort is looking very lovely tonight.'

He did not notice I was shaking but passed in front of me and giving my niece his arm led her solemnly around the table. She smiled faintly, triumphantly, as she took her seat. Claude proposed a toast. My niece had reached the age of twenty-one and we should drink to her future. I raised my glass, trying to erase the sight of Agnès at the other end of the table. She sat like a queen in Angeline's wedding dress, tossing her pretty smiles at the men who hung on every word. I barely heard their talk of St Pierre and the volcano, wishing that she were gone from my house, that she had never come here.

'One man survived,' said Claude to Agnès.

'Aunt Lily told me the story.'

'There's always a lone survivor, evidently.'

'Ended his days in a circus.'

'You're making it up.'

'Yes he did. Barnum's travelling circus.'

'He was under sentence of death.'

'Reprieved, of course.'

'That's only fair.'

'Thirty-thousand dead and a grown man in a circus.'

'There was an election at the time.'

'I know. Who won?'

'Who won what?'

'The election.'

'Everyone died, dammit.'

'Except Ciparis . . .'

'I don't believe you.'

David Taverner suddenly leant towards me and said, 'Madame, how very odd. I feel I've been here before.'

I looked at him blankly. 'But you have indeed, been here before. Several times.'

'I mean . . . this evening. We've been through it once already. What they've been saying.'

'Perhaps they repeat themselves. I can't help you, I'm afraid. I really wasn't paying attention.'

Claude looked at Agnès and said, 'You know they call this *le pays des revenants*.' His smile lingered. 'The land of those who return,' he added in English for Taverner's benefit.

'And ghosts. . .'

Did I say that, or did Agnès?

We finished the meal and drank our coffee where we sat under the stars. As Claude had remarked, Agnès looked exceedingly pretty. Her blonde hair had slipped from its ribbon so that every now and then she tossed back her head, causing her breasts to rise from the corsage of her dress.

Claude's eyes strayed continually in her direction. He would shake his head and smile to himself in wonderment then make some abstruse comment to the Englishman which served to deepen the latter's unease. I tried to talk to Taverner about his people and was told that his father, a waterworks engineer, had retired to Scotland and that his mother had run off with a Lebanese doctor, divorced his father, remarried and settled in Cyprus. It seemed kindest to cease my enquiries. One must make allowances for the unfortunate circumstances of others.

As for Agnès, I could not excuse her behaviour, flouting conventions and respect for other people's property. I was not to know that she would pay dearly for her transgressions. We cannot be prescient at all times. I decided to talk to the girl in the morning and threaten to send her back to Gustave (alone) if she did not behave herself properly.

The speakers down my valley had long since ceased to parade their empty phrases like packaged goods in a supermarket. A wind had blown up and the trees creaked above our heads, murmuring faintly in unison. The night air was fresh and cool. Agnès went inside to fetch a shawl and on her return was most upset to discover she had lost the pendant her mother had given her. The four of us felt about the grass, rather feebly in view of the darkness. When Agnès stepped towards the undergrowth she was startled by a disembodied face peering out from the edge of the plantation. She called out in fear, something about a 'daughter'. I made no sense of such an odd remark. David Taverner stood by her side. She pointed in one direction, then another. We were all confused. Suddenly the Englishman dived into the bushes and after a scuffle returned bearing Yvette, Eveline's demented child, who scowled at us like a demon. In her hand she clutched Agnès's pendant which had to be forcibly removed. I summoned Eveline to take the child away.

The episode cast a shadow over the evening and my headache worsened so that when Agnès suggested we play some records on the veranda and dance on the grass I went to bed, catching a final glimpse of the three from the window of my upstairs room. Agnès and Taverner danced to the lively tunes of my mazurkas watched by Claude who sat to one side and beat his hands in time to the music. I pulled the shutters and fell asleep at once in spite of the sounds of laughter below.

When I awoke it was dark, very dark. Our nights are blacker than yours, more intense. I cannot have slept for more than an hour or two. When I was accustomed to the darkness I rose to fetch a glass of water. As I opened the door I thought I heard voices. I listened again. The house was silent though the stairs creaked at my passage. A light at the back of the house shone inwards along the polished floors of the corridor. I checked the kitchen first, which was empty, and the work-room and André's study. The sitting-room looked strangely large, an effect no doubt of the dark night. As quietly as possible I released the metal bolts on the door. Outside the insects spoke among themselves and a candle flickered fitfully in its glass, almost at an end. I had imagined everything. We all hear voices from time to time in our private labyrinths.

The candle went out. I moved back towards the door and then I heard it again. Those sounds. There was someone in Agnès's room. They did not speak but I heard those sounds and I *knew*.

8

HAD I PUT a stop to her disgraceful behaviour would Agnès have been saved? Would she walk among us still? I should certainly have suppressed her fanciful notions of Angeline. The girl was quite simply a whore: not my expression, I assure you, I repeat only what people said about her. The marriage she contracted was out of the question. The fellow worked on André's land in some lowly capacity. It could not be permitted. André acted in the girl's best interests knowing she would suffer unhappiness for a time but hearts and souls mend quickly and he offered to send her to Europe to stay with my family. The girl refused. In disobedience of my husband's orders she continued to meet the man secretly in the hurricane shelter, away from prying eyes, and by the time these trysts were known it was much too late. Angeline bore him a half-breed daughter who died a short time afterwards.

As soon as her condition became obvious Angeline was cloistered in the house. Although we had dismissed the servants, they rumoured of dreadful happenings, our good name sullied. I could not face the talk, the insinuations, and felt as much a prisoner as Angeline. Maryse and Sophie tried to rebuild the bridges between us but André's heart was turned and I doubt if he ever directly addressed his sister again. It was he who forbade the taking of any photographs of Angeline.

I should have told all this to Agnès and made her see reason. The girl would have understood why the subject pained me. Until Angeline's disgrace we had formed a happy household leading cheerful lives in the broad light of day. Angeline's story would have taught Agnès a lesson, that one cannot depart from conventions without paying for the privilege. But I could not bring myself to speak of such matters as I could not bring myself to ask about the man in her bedroom. There are certain questions one cannot pose of relatives and friends.

Instead of talking to Agnès as I had intended I stayed in my room, feigning a migraine which meant I could see no one, a prohibition that included Agnès. The girl rose late, I heard her creeping about the house, then Eveline announced she had gone to Fort de France where she would remain until nightfall as the Préfet was scheduled to deliver an important address on the Savannah. Once she had gone I dressed but did not have the spirit to visit Claude in his house by the sea. I needed time to think how I should deal with this girl who, though I loved her in my fashion, seemed ready to betray my trust at the slightest opportunity.

The *Savane* is constructed for emptiness and chance meetings by the statue of Josephine, not for the crowds which poured in that night to hear the Préfet speak. Their numbers and the brooding silence should have warned Agnès that something was wrong and that a white girl cannot melt into darkness. She noticed nothing unusual. As she had arrived rather late she stood on the edge of the surging crowd with her back to the trees.

On a makeshift stage erected by the seafront several leading citizens had already taken their seats under the floodlights which illuminated a battery of microphones. The Préfet was expected at seven. When he had not arrived by half-past the temper of the crowd was unpleasant but still as silent as night. At last his car was sighted inching its way down the rue de la Liberté. Crowds flocked into the roadway and even a Préfet cannot mow down his people without immediate recall to France. So he made the last few hundred metres on foot, surrounded by thickset bodyguards who clove a path through indiscriminate humanity. The Préfet clearly disliked the sight which met him from the stage: black faces in the black night emitting a tangible hostility. He spoke hurriedly with the Commissaire de Police, who comes from Bordeaux and swaggers unpleasantly. The policeman indicated the holster on his hip. Somewhat reassured, the Préfet started to speak, of destiny and freedom, rolling his fine sentences above the heads of the crowd like the barrack-room orators of St Antoine. At the exact point in his speech when he moved to embrace moral certitudes the electricity failed, doubtless by design. The Préfet's beautiful phrase was cut in half: no power, no microphone. His floodlight was extinguished in the same instant. No one could see a thing.

The leaders of this 'revolt' were well organised. With one accord the crowd produced candles which burnt under the stars: a terrifying spectacle. The flames twitched in the wind that blew from the sea, bringing with them the *voudou* gods and the sound of feet stamping on earth, a low steady rumbling that grew louder and more intense, the sound of Africa and forgotten continents, the sound of a people who had elected at last to say 'no' to our dominion. Indeed, a few placards appeared above the heads. *Non*, they declared, and again, *Non*. (We are always being asked to vote 'yes' or 'no' to some bright notion concocted in the *métropole*.) The placards provided an unequivocal response to all the questions we had asked in the past and the ones we might ask in future. Do you want our roads, our economic miracles? *Non*. Our schools, our engineers, our advisers? *Non*. Our Cartesian dualism? *Non*. Our language? *Non*. Our interpretation of liberty? *Non*, *non*, *non*.

When the slaves revolted, they wanted not to win but to make their masters afraid. The crowd moved closer to the stage from which the Préfet, his wife, and other notables made an undignified exit down a ladder at the back that led to the sea-wall. They hurried away unmolested as the crowd pushed forward intent on destruction. According to the newspapers the Chief of Police showed commendable bravery and for several minutes kept the crowd at bay, shooting his pistol into the air, although Agnès maintained that the demented figure on stage was a black man saluting his victory not a white man protecting his skin. The official version is preferable to all concerned because three people were wounded by bullets: a boy at the side of the stage shot in the face and two women hit by ricochets as they returned home.

Agnès remembered little of how she escaped. For a time she stayed pressed against the trees as the crowd swarmed past – wild eyes and teeth that snapped in her face. In front of her, a group of children, shouting madly, were snatched up and passed over heads. A woman clawed at her shirt. Men closed in. They waved sticks and chanted, horrible chants – she saw nothing but the whites of their eyes. Sirens screamed in the distance. Smoke then flames rose from the shattered stage as the police charged from several directions at once, wielding batons like flails that threshed all heads in their path. Grown men rushed at each other, collided, fell to the ground, were trampled on. Agnès was carried forward, lifted off her feet, unable to fight against the tide. She was scratched, jostled, pushed, felt herself falling, was caught by the crush of bodies that carried her onwards. Then the lights came back. A madman danced in the flames. Smoke hung above the crowd and sirens wailed at the crossroads. By now she had clawed her way to the edge of the crowd which streamed down the rue de la Liberté towards the Boulevard Alfassa and the Baie des Flamands. On the seafront they stoned the Office du Tourisme as well as the Centre des Métiers d'Art, the Monument aux Morts, and the Statue d'Esnambuc. The crowd had lost all reason.

Agnès, meanwhile, was deposited like jetsam on the steps of the Hôtel Impératrice. The crowd passed by and she watched the police charge helpless bystanders as the acrid smell of tear-gas blew across the Savannah from the Avenue des Caraïbes.

The world had gone mad and Agnès saw it all. She heard a voice behind her. Someone called her name. Slowly she turned as a man at the other side of the café rose to his feet. She saw him only as a blur, a menacing shape that moved towards her across the empty room. Panic returned. She descended a couple of steps, preferring the madness outside to the terror within, but as she turned she tripped and fell backwards in the street.

The man who so terrified my niece was Claude who had calmly observed the spectacle from the terrace of the Hôtel Impératrice. Heedless of any possible danger he picked her up and carried her senseless body through the back streets of

Fort de France to his car parked behind the Hôtel de Ville, where the girl revived enough to recognise she was safe and in good hands. He wrapped her in a blanket and brought her home to me.

This was our second riot within a year. Although the material damage was considerable – and hospitals had to patch up a number of broken heads – we should be thankful that no one was killed. A local newspaper editor initiated a collection for the restitution of flower beds around the Savannah, crushed by panicked feet. Donations flowed in and no one spared a thought for the victims.

The city returned to normal. Police patrols herded up anyone who strayed into the streets so that by morning the jails overflowed. Rumour suggested that back in the *métropole* the President of the Republic had dispatched a warship, though it is doubtful what a ship could achieve when the troubles were on land not sea. In the grey light of dawn the chief remnant of our 'small riot' – in addition to crushed flower beds, broken windows and sore heads – was a red-painted banner draped nonchalantly around the breasts of Josephine. *Black pimps, white whore* it proclaimed to a city which slept. The banner was quickly removed.

David Taverner, who had come to Martinique in search of a story, was in another part of the island when the riot occurred owing to the intervention of Madame Ségovie who, after my party, had tracked him down to the Hôtel des Innocents and insisted on a meeting with her husband, the Secretary-General of the Union of Proletarian Workers. (Taverner had been unwise enough to reveal to the woman that he wished to meet everyone of consequence during his visit.)

As the crowds engaged in pitched battles with the police Taverner sat in a room full of bespectacled young men, up in

Macouba, listening to speaker after speaker denounce the cultural imperialism of France. At the end they linked hands to sing the *Internationale*, and Taverner was annoyed to discover he had forgotten the tune. On the return journey, beyond Lorrain, Ségovie's car developed an oil leak and Taverner spent an uncomfortable half hour under the engine, lying on his back in the mud. No one offered to pay for the damage to his trousers. Despite this mishap, he had found the Secretary-General agreeable and they parted on reasonable terms.

At the hotel Taverner went straight upstairs to bed. He was woken at five in the morning by an irate proprietor clad in a towel, who said he was required on the telephone. The news editor of Taverner's paper had received word over the wires of a serious disturbance in Fort de France and wanted to know what was going on. Taverner stalled for time by saying that he was putting the finishing touches to his story which he would telex within the hour. As soon as the conversation was finished he threw on some clothes and drove to Fort de France with Léopold, equally bleary-eyed, where he purchased the first edition of *France-Antilles*.

The front page story was obsessively concerned with flowers. Taverner made a number of telephone calls and was able to trace at least one eyewitness to the riot whose impressions were translated into Taverner's own. The story was sent off three hours late and Taverner returned to Vauclin, aware that he had acquitted himself badly. He resolved to cut Madame Ségovie dead, the next time he saw her, and was fortified by the belief that someone else was to blame. He had not suspected that Agnès might have provided an excellent source for his story. He was not to know this until after she disappeared, as he never saw her again.

As soon as Claude had brought Agnès home from the riot, her livid scratches and tattered clothing concealed by a blanket, I put her to bed where she clung to my neck and buried her head on my shoulder, then requested a candle *à tout hasard*. It is possible I felt Agnès had received her just deserts – the world of men is a cruel place in which one cannot walk at will. But the sight of this defenceless waif curled up among the bedclothes reminded me that Gustave had entrusted her to my care and all thought of further punishment was gone. I grew almost to like her in those quiet moments, while I watched her sleep.

Outside her door Claude enquired anxiously after Agnès. He was restless that night, padding the length of the house, sitting down only to stand up immediately, thrusting his hands into his pockets and jangling coins which jarred my nerves. He talked in rapid bursts – about Agnès and myself, about the riot whose futility appalled him. The forces of law and order, he said, would simply tighten their grip on a timid people that had yet to discover a soul. I tried to supply the gaps in his conversation but was powerless against the tiredness which seeped through my body: mind and limbs exhausted by the turmoil of that endless day.

I must have fallen asleep because when I started awake Claude sat before me on the veranda, staring towards the slatted window of my niece's room. Disoriented, I cried out in fear. Just so had André sat for many years watching his sister Angeline behind the shutters, with just that bitter look in his eyes, love crossed with yearning, gentleness, despair, in the days before the girl's disgrace when he could bear the sight of her no more.

Claude turned at my cry. Had I been dreaming? A nightmare? I wanted him to leave. In my moment of waking I had remembered and cried aloud in pain. Do not dig deeply into the hearts of families if you wish to contain their rottenness.

André and Angeline ... Fairest of all, he claimed, far prettier than I. They used to talk about the pair of them. Such love between a brother and a sister. Exemplary affection. Only I knew better. With child I saw her as a monster. He gave her even that which he denied me. The man she wished to wed, I thought they had invented him to hide their wickedness. But then she killed my fears. Thrust into the world a half-black baby to silence forever the hateful rumours that destroyed our lives. And André never spoke to her again. Shut himself away where none might reach him, within the coldness of his tired heart. He died a broken man, all trust betrayed. God rest his soul and bring him peace at last.

This other man had come to take his place. He would transport me to another continent where I might live once more. I asked for brandy and swallowed greedily while Claude fussed at my side, attempting to locate the cause of my distress. I wished him gone to face my phantoms alone.

Throughout the night my husband stayed with me. Perched on my bed and clawed my withered soul. He would not let me sleep, sat like a judge, hard and dispassionate, and tried me for the sins of others. That look in his eyes, a mask I might never penetrate. The way he set his chin, so many gestures which revealed his heart. Snapshots from happier days do not make a lifetime. So much is absent. So much cut out because it hurts us to remember. I once asked God to take him away.

André was not like this. He was a good man. A rock within our insular community. The rest is unimportant. The day he brought me home to the island, into the arms of his family. The same day Angeline said sneeringly, 'So this is what you bought in Paris.' I heard them. I stood outside the door. He reasoned with her but she cried and cried, called me a foolish woman, a trinket, until he gave her comfort and not me. Left me outside to overhear their whisperings.

Those times – they do not matter. Voices on the veranda, weaving their worlds in which I had no place. His other sisters, Sophie and Maryse, good people who refused to be my friends, who exiled me from life, a stranger in their midst unable to return home knowing how they would speak of me afterwards. Or not speak, far worse: a woman who had chanced upon them and was gone, who might have been a ghost. I could not bear that fate. I stayed. I had no choice. I heard their footsteps creaking in the long dark nights. And voices, always voices. Cajoling, pleading, playing, spinning fantasies behind closed doors. I stayed among them and outlived them all.

Dawn came and I was broken. We had fought so bitterly, André and I, his shadow furnishing my room, displacing the images I held so dear, that when he left I felt more alone than I had ever been. I reached for the portrait which since his death has graced my bedside. A brave young man in uniform with such a handsome smile. A good man, I told myself, as if his goodness could depend on words. The man who brought me here and shaped my life. We cannot excise the basis of our existence and though we live in dreams we must believe in them. I held him to me, remembering how he was when we first met, the deep-set smile behind his piercing eyes, his tales of adventure and human endeavour. I loved him then and always shall, no matter how he hurt me. He captured me – willingly – and cannot harm me now. I hold him in my hands and watch the smile deepen. Angeline fell with other men, not André. The girl was damned by us and by the world.

This knowledge brought me peace. Sinking to my knees I prayed sincerely that the scourge of distrust might spread no further, and that my fight with André would be the last.

The stillness after storms is always remarkable. The air regains a deeper limpidity and one can breathe again, filling one's lungs with hope. I gloried in the freshness of the morning and felt a spreading of wings.

Several hours after sunrise Claude telephoned to enquire after the invalids. I laughed at his question, having forgotten Agnès and her recent ordeal. Locked within my own battles it was as if I had mislaid my relatives. When I said this Claude wondered aloud if I were really well. Of course I was well, and full of hope. Choosing his words carefully Claude asked me not to mention the riot to Agnès's parents, at least not her involvement – if they knew of her danger they would seek her return. 'Most probably,' I said, 'which is precisely the point. You told me to look after her better, remember?'

'I was referring to Agnès and David Taverner.'

'Oh that,' I said, 'I don't think we need worry about the Englishman.' Claude sounded distant and suspecting he wished to return to his work I said goodbye. He asked again if I were really well. I remember feeling rather impatient with him, and disconcerted by his latest request, but he asked me to trust him, which I did, of course, with all my heart, setting aside my woman's instincts because it is only right to trust one's fellow men.

Shortly afterwards, Taverner telephoned to speak to Agnès. He had been ordered to leave the island by his editor, who had faulted his eyewitness account of the riot in a number of important aspects, and he wanted to say goodbye.

In her room Agnès sat by the window looking dreamily across the lawn. She had not responded to my knock and scarcely noticed my presence. When I said that David Taverner wanted to speak to her she shook her head violently and said that to see or even speak to him would be 'unfair'. She returned her gaze to the trees, obviously wishing to be alone. Taverner was to telephone several times in the next few days and invariably received the same response.

Agnès's behaviour disturbed me. Suspecting she suffered the effects of delayed shock I called Dr Marignot. He came immediately, prodded her, pressed her, checked her heartbeat, pulse rate, blood pressure and declared her pefectly well apart from her pallor for which he prescribed a sensible programme of diet and exercise which the girl ignored. She stayed in her room most of the time, and ate little, much to Eveline's shame.

I left Agnès to herself during the day and at night tried to entertain her with cheerful reminiscences to which I got little response. The crickets made more noise than she did and I grew to dread our lugubrious dinners when the sounds of the jungle closed in and we were thrown to the mercy of each other's company.

Once or twice I knocked at her door, receiving no answer, and one morning took her a letter from Louis Gavron. The room was empty and I thought nothing more about it.

We saw little of Claude in the days that followed as he worked studiously on the new collection of poems to be presented at Madame Ségovie's evening; having accepted the invitation he wanted to do his best. I respected his desire for privacy but sorely missed our conversations in the late afternoons which had given shape and purpose to my life. Because of his seclusion I visited André more frequently, as I had in the old days, and never once forgot my flowers. Each visit I asked for his forgiveness, assuring him that I never doubted his integrity and if he acted harshly towards me it was only his manner. I dusted his photograph and swept away the spiders which nested in the corners of his grave. Soon there was room for no more bouquets and Father

Thomas suggested his church would welcome any flowers I could spare. I agreed on condition that he left the lilies. So André had two visitors each day: first myself and then Father Thomas's housekeeper who trotted up the path to remove a selection of my latest offerings. We often crossed each other at the gates and stopped to pass the time of day.

On the third or fourth day of my new regime I arrived at the cemetery around midday and was most disturbed to find André's sepulchre already resplendent with a freshly-picked spray of scarlet hibiscus. The sight filled me with dread. I could think of no one who might wish to pay their respects to my long-dead husband. Agnès was locked in her room – the young have in any case no time for sentiment – and the dead do not give each other flowers. Perhaps I had already visited André?

I drove out to the headland above Claude's house, parking my car by the statue of Our Lady of Guadeloupe who stretches out her hands to the waves as if she might quieten the seas. Warm winds blew in my face and I thought of Claude at his desk, struggling to find the words for silence. In the distance loomed the Ilet St Aubin, named after a minor branch of André's family, an uninhabited crop of stark grey rocks topped with wind-swept trees.

To my surprise – and indignation – I caught a glimpse of two figures at Claude's window below. While I was happy to accept his need for solitude I assumed that others would too and that if he received visitors their number should include myself. I locked the car and walked angrily down the footpath, dropping into the sullen heat. By the time I reached his house it was shuttered and empty; the light often plays tricks on tired eyes. I pushed a note under his door to say that I had passed and missed him, then walked along the beach before returning home.

Agnès, as usual, was locked in her room and refused to

answer my knock. The stillness of the house enervated me, not that I wished for bustle and noisy laughter, having spent too many hours alone. But if someone shares my house they must respect conventions, speak when spoken to, appear at mealtimes and contribute to useful human intercourse. I resolved therefore that the girl should accompany me on an outing and I took her again to St Pierre, driving over the mountains past the Trace des Jésuites and down through Fond St Denis, hoping to jolt her with memories of that other day we had taken the same route – her birthday that ended so disgracefully. Agnès sat mutely at my side. I doubt if she noticed the splendid mountain views from Trou Matelots, the Forêt du Morne des Olives, the Porte d'Enfer or the Rivière du Jardin des Plantes. We parked by the cathedral, a gaunt and massive construction, and walked up the rue Victor Hugo to the volcanic museum where we looked again at calcified tea cups and all the other banal reminders of that day when St Pierre was wiped off the face of the earth. Still she was silent. I took her back to the beach where we walked towards the rocks and Agnès unearthed a pile of bones in the dull grey sand.

'Your friend,' she said suddenly, 'Señor Cerda. He says that when people die they go to the town of the angels. *El pueblo de los angeles*. The words sound better in Spanish, don't you think Aunt Lily?'

Without waiting for an answer she walked towards the quiet sea. I knew then that I had been foolish in turning to Dr Marignot because it was not her body that needed help but her soul.

9

IN THE SHADE of my room I sit on the big wooden bed and look once more at Agnès's diary in which her generous handwriting sprawls from page to page, one thought running into the next without order or discipline. Many passages I know by heart having studied it assiduously in the vain hope that one more reading will deliver up its secrets. It is hidden in the marqueterie cabinet beside my bed – held back from the rest of Agnès's effects which I returned to France as I wanted to spare Gustave and Marie-Louise the full knowledge of their daughter's waywardness. To read it gives me such pain. I am my own executioner. She cannot really have hated me that much . . . *I* was the one who suffered.

On several occasions I have taken the diary to her favourite haunts, including Taverner's hotel where I have sat downstairs in that execrable bar surrounded by ill-kempt men who look at me with ironic surprise. But I come no closer to understanding how she felt. The task defeats me as so much is unrecorded. Take the day of the riot, for example, a blank page cannot elucidate the truth. I should put the thing away for good and plague myself no more.

But somewhere lies the key . . . If only I could read between the lines I might discover what really happened, and when . . .

18 April

A strange feeling of calm has returned. All is for the best in the best of possible worlds. But do we ever learn from experience? I'm fed with words and starved of example. At a distance I followed Aunt Lily to the cemetery where André lies smothered by flowers. With his photograph and little crucifix he seems quite at home. I wanted her to see me but she was so busy talking to her famous ghost she had no time for the living.

19 April

David can't recognise a lost cause when it stares him in the face. Sometimes I feel I have the fever, and walk through cold, northern mists between the shoreline and the still, quiet sea, while the next minute I'm up among the clouds with the rainbows, so light I can fly – a tall white lady half-glimpsed between the railings of desire. Come to me tonight and tell me I shall always be your lady of midnight.

Yvette is a monster. She follows me quite openly a few steps behind. I've given up trying to be friends. She watches me and waits. I'd hit her if I got the chance.

20 April

Louis sent me a card for my birthday, an afterthought, not even a letter. I don't care. I walk a tightrope high above the world and can't possibly fall. You'll find wild orchids in my breasts, lost continents submerged between my thighs.

Eveline told me of the ghost that eats bad children in the night. It comes down from the hills and tears them apart, crunching the bones and snapping off their heads. It likes their livers best which are kept to the last. She wants to frighten me and doesn't realise I'm invincible.

21 April

I hate my aunt. We sit at her polished table with its china and glass and ridiculous ceremony while Eveline waits on us disapprovingly then disappears to the kitchen where she starts her singing. The world is falling apart and we exchange polite conversation.

Today she took me to St Pierre where I found bones on the beach. Human bones. She's wrong if she thinks a little sight-seeing can put me right. I won't be mended like a broken toy. On the way back she told me the full story of Angeline and expected me to be shocked by her behaviour. I wasn't. Angeline was magnificent. I thought of her daughter and cried for her when I was alone. I hate the sunsets. We sit on the veranda and slip into a strange grey world followed by nothingness. I hate everything. I'm alone and frightened and nobody cares. They spy on me, play with me, tear me apart, and then abandon me.

22 April

The clasp on my diary is broken. Everything is known and nothing excused. But your sex is a torch which I shall carry through the world to illuminate my darkness.

23 April
I'm lost in the overgrown gardens of a château at night, running up and down steps in a long white dress with full skirts that I must lift off the ground, otherwise I fall. I hear the sound of Mozart and minuets, and everywhere fountains, the noise of gently flowing water which pours from the mouths of cherubs and dolphins. All the time I'm running with dainty little steps in white satin shoes and am not in the least afraid.

24 April
On the grass under the cassia trees I saw two butterflies with black velvet wings that hovered near my hands. I could reach out and touch them, they were so close. Eveline says they're called *papillon-lanmò*, death's butterflies, and that to see them brings good luck.

There is no entry for the 25th of April in Agnès's diary. Her cry for help echoes in my room like the sound of the *siffleur de montagne*, but no one answered. We were deaf as well as blind.

The 25th of April, you see, was the day of the taking of Agnès.

10

ON THE morning of the 25th I awoke before dawn from a terrible dream. I dreamed of the desecration of André's grave. His headstone smashed with an axe. Dead flowers strewn about the ground. The plinth defaced with crude and vulgar words. Agnès did it – in my dream at least. Laid waste the stones and drew the sign in blood. She did it and at the same time did not do it, as is the way of dreams, while I stood helpless. Men would repair the damage and I would pay them. There are always men who will do things if the price is right.

I had to quit the house. It was an evil place to harbour such fantasies. With the quickening of light I walked to the rocks beyond the sugar cane from where you can look down across our blue-green seas. The beauty of that quiet morning failed to touch me. All around was dead, as if they had picked clean my landscape and left behind the greyness of its bones. I stood there for an hour at least, willing God to send me His punishment. Was I a fugitive, a vagabond marked with His sign so all might track me down? Was I wicked, as they were? Had He rejected me? I could not return home, not yet. It was much too soon. I watched the dawn creeping up from the horizon, willing the magic to return once more. In my heart I blamed Agnès who had exhumed the spectre of Angeline, in looks and deeds, and threatened to destroy my past. And yet she was my brother's daughter, and I her keeper. Like Eveline my saints were all confused. If only He would send me a sign to show He listened. To show He knew I suffered and was thus absolved from blame. To bring me peace. He mocked me with the silence of that morning. Quietened the dogs and stopped their throats. I turned my heart away. When darkness calls the sin is always yours.

Below me, by the seafront, the lights of St Antoine went out one by one. Morning had come. I thought I heard a car in the distance, somewhere near my house. The engine died. I waited several minutes. The car stuttered into life again. That was a sign, of sorts. I knew it was time to leave, not wishing my absence to be noticed.

The walk seemed endless. As I turned into the drive I heard the faint ringing of the telephone and slowed my pace. The ringing stopped when I reached the steps but began again when I crossed the threshold. Like a fool I answered it and have often wondered what would have happened, had I not done so.

David Taverner called from the airport. It was the date of his departure and his flight was delayed. This was fortunate, he said, because Léopold had failed to collect him as promised and he had been forced to flag down a taxi with only minutes to spare. He asked to speak to Agnès. I said at once it was much too early as my niece was still asleep, but he insisted. Her door was shut and I received no reply. You must understand this was not unusual. As I returned to the telephone, Eveline hurried from the kitchen. Excitedly she said that Agnès had left the house half an hour earlier in the company of two men. They wore hats and she saw them only fleetingly from behind. She had thought the episode odd but assured me that Agnès had gone with the men of her own accord. Taverner overheard this conversation – I could not prevent it – but seemed unable or unwilling to grasp that Agnès had gone. He asked if she normally left the house at such an early hour and whether Eveline had recognised the men who accompanied her.

'No, I rarely see my niece before midday and no, Eveline did not recognise either of the men.'

He was silent then asked hesitantly, 'She really is out?'

'Yes,' I snapped, 'I'm not in the habit of lying.'

'Forgive me, Madame. That wasn't what I meant at all. But she's been out rather a lot recently. To me, I mean. I think she's been avoiding me.'

'That may be, but this time out means out.'

'You really have no idea where she might have gone?'

'None whatsoever,' I replied firmly, forcing Taverner to say his reluctant goodbyes to *me*, not Agnès, and I wished I had shown more kindness as we would not meet again.

On that point I was mistaken. Only an hour later I was sitting on the lawn watching Pépé hacking at my flowerbeds when a taxi drew up with Claude and David Taverner. The two men were clearly discomforted as they walked towards me across the grass and I tried to conquer my premonition that something was wrong.

Claude kissed my cheek and the Englishman and I shook hands. Taverner carried a small leather suitcase, rather scuffed, which he transferred clumsily to his left hand before taking my own. His grip was firm although he seemed unable to look me in the eye, and bared his teeth in an effort to smile. Claude carried an extra chair from the veranda.

'What has brought you both here?' I asked, looking from one to the other. Neither answered, so I went on, 'M. Taverner, I thought you had left us. . .'

'Agnès,' said Taverner, ignoring my implicit question, 'has she returned?'

'Why do you ask? I don't wish to be rude but. . .'

'Those men,' he broke in, 'the ones who took her away.'

'I'm afraid you exaggerate. No one *took* Agnès anywhere. We have Eveline's word. She went of her own free will.' I hoped they could not hear the beating of my heart. 'I expect she'll return any minute. I'm sorry I can't ask you to stay,' I added hastily, staring malevolently at his suitcase.

'I hope you're right, Madame. With all my heart. Because you see . . . Oh my God . . .' His voice trailed off.

I turned to Claude who sat quietly by my side, hands clasped in his lap, watching us both and missing nothing. 'Can you enlighten me?' I said. 'M. Taverner seems somewhat confused. Is he quite all right?'

Claude threw back his head and laughed. The echo rang around the trees. It shocked me to hear him laughing so blatantly at what I had said. He stopped suddenly and the laughter went out from his eyes. 'Our friend will stay,' he said with a shrug, 'until the little one returns.'

'Madame, I'm terribly sorry,' said Taverner. 'Your niece . . . I think . . .'

'What do you think, Monsieur?'

'My newspaper . . . I've been given new instructions to stay here until . . .'

'Until when? And what on earth has this to do with Agnès? I assume there *is* a connection?'

He nodded bleakly then blurted out, 'I think she's disappeared. No, worse than that. I think she's been kidnapped.'

I shut my eyes and felt the world slip away.

'*Kidnapped*? Are you mad?'

'Madame, I . . .'

'Explain yourself, young man. How did you arrive at this ridiculous conclusion?'

'She was expected somewhere. This morning. And never arrived. We waited until we were sure.'

'Where was she expected? And who are "we"?'

The men glanced at each other. I thought I saw Claude shake his head. 'Tell me where,' I insisted. 'You seem extraordinarily well-informed about my household. Agnès said you might have been a spy.'

The Englishman reddened. Claude smiled fleetingly and said, 'I think you're being a little hard on the man, Alicia. He's only doing his job. He is a reporter, after all.'

'Then he should stick to the facts,' I retorted. We fell silent. My disbelief in Taverner's story lay between us like a gauntlet and I tried my utmost to appear calm.

We sat in uneasy silence when Eveline appeared across the lawn bringing coffee for my guests. Without asking permission the Englishman questioned her about what she had seen: two unidentified men in hats (back view only) and my niece who waved briefly from a disappearing car. Taverner recorded the details in a notebook in spite of my looks which made it plain I considered his action seditious.

'And Mlle Montfort,' said Taverner, 'how did she seem to you?'

'Same as ever, you know.' Eveline had unaccountably slipped into the informal style of address. 'I tell her often, she'll come to no good.'

'That will do, Eveline,' I said curtly.

'I only say what he asks,' grumbled Eveline. 'That girl, just lately, she brings trouble.'

I glanced at Claude who was staring at his hands. He raised his head and when he saw me looking at him, opened his lips to speak but obviously thought better of it.

'You may go now,' I said to Eveline.

'Only what he asks, Madame. Nothing more.'

Eveline went back to the house. The sun circling round the trees shone directly in my eyes. We moved our chairs. Taverner continued to write in his notebook until my patience broke.

'Don't you understand anything?' I said. 'If you're right about Agnès, *if*, I repeat, surely the first rule is silence. Give the perpetrators of such acts a breath of publicity and they strangle you on the spot.'

'You mean Agnès . . .'

'I do not mean Agnès, I mean us.'

'I'm a journalist . . .'

'I have only your word for it. If we're not careful they'll all be at our throats. What have you done?' I cried, aware that my voice had risen. 'Why have you interfered in our lives?'

Taverner looked shaken by my outburst. He thought for a moment, then asked, 'Did they leave a note, perhaps, giving their demands?'

'I don't know who "they" are, and if they had left a note I certainly wouldn't tell you. I think you've caused enough trouble already.'

'What do you mean, Madame?'

'I understand you gave Agnès a gun.' Claude looked up in surprise. Of course he had not read her diary in which she revealed it was the gun wrapped in brown paper which passed between them near the statue of Josephine. Taverner swore softly to himself.

'You put guns in the hands of children and innocents.'

'It wasn't loaded, I promise you.'

'What difference does that make? How could you be so stupid?'

'I was being followed, Madame. I had to get rid of it.'

'So you gave it to Agnès. Just like that.'

'She couldn't shoot anyone.'

'The only person I can think of shooting is you, Monsieur. Your business here is finished. Guns, indeed. If anything happens to Agnès I shall hold you personally responsible.' I stood up and Taverner jumped to his feet. 'Madame, may I say how desperately sorry I am that this should happen . . .'

'That won't get us very far,' I replied, ignoring his outstretched hand.

We watched him disappear down the drive struggling with his suitcase. Once or twice he looked back over his shoulder. When he had gone I burst into tears. The events of that morning had proved too much: the dream, the silence, the dead, grey lands. And now Agnès . . . Claude stroked my hand and tried to comfort me. He held me close when the police arrived, eight of them in three cars heralded by the whine of sirens. One man parked on the grass and was quickly rebuked. It appears the Englishman had telephoned them as well as his newspaper and I wondered angrily at his impertinence.

They trooped through my house and swarmed over Agnès's room with their cameras, their fingerprint dust, all the paraphernalia of detection. Then they took down our stories. Claude remained in the background. *No, I had no reason to suspect Agnès had been kidnapped. No, I had seen and heard nothing. Yes, she was perfectly happy. No, there was no note, from her or anyone.*

The police asked for her photograph. I have an album

full, sent by Gustave at regular intervals, but as she had matured in recent months I gave them the print which Taverner had taken on the beach near Ste Anne. Satisfied, they returned to their cars. Pépé stood by the house, staring open-mouthed. He caught my look and in a frenzy began sweeping leaves from the gravel.

Claude wished to return to work. We walked to the gates, stepping through shadows to escape the full heat of the sun. There was so much I wanted to ask him but I felt confused by the sudden turn of events, and more than a little afraid, so we kept to the facts and discussed whether the political situation was volatile enough to support Taverner's theory of a kidnap. Claude was non-committal though convinced that something untoward had happened. That much was clear: my niece was gone. We stood by the gates. Claude wore one of the suits on which Agnès had remarked in her diary. It looked as if he had slept in it all night. His face was unrefreshed, grey and waxed around the edges, and I thought for the first time that he was older than I. I asked when he had last seen Agnès.

He replied without hesitation, 'After the riot, when I brought her home.'

He held both my hands and I looked deeply into his dear, remembered face.

'We'll find her,' he promised. Then he kissed me and was gone. I stayed at the gates until his noble figure had disappeared.

My house was utterly still. I went into Agnès's room where the shutters were drawn and the darkness held me in its hands. I sat quietly until Eveline returned. She threw open the shutters, bustled about the room, tidied away the clothes Agnès had worn the day before.

'Shall I make the bed, Madame?'

'Later,' I said absently.

Eveline watched me from the doorway. 'The little one will return,' she said, 'I know . . .' Even my maid addressed me as a child.

'Go now,' I said, and she left me alone.

I opened the chest of drawers. My niece's clothes were in considerable disorder, mixed up with books and make-up and scraps of paper. In the top drawer I found her diary as well as several letters from Marie-Louise and one, written by an obviously male hand, that had been torn in two. I presumed it was from Louis Gavron. Under the mattress I found Taverner's gun, where it had always been. Our police are not especially efficient. I held the gun in my hands. It felt heavy and the barrel looked crooked. Aiming at the window I pulled the trigger. Nothing happened. It was unloaded as Taverner had said.

'Monsieur Poincaret?'

I gripped the telephone receiver tightly with both hands. Having decided to place the call, it was important not to fail now.

'*Oui*,' he replied, then cleared his throat. I held the receiver at some distance from my ear, tempted to replace it quickly and let events take their course.

'Allo?' he said several times. I drew a breath. 'Madame de Ste Croix speaking,' I said slowly. His voice took on a new obsequiousness.

'*Enchanté*, Madame, how can I help you?'

'I have a problem, Monsieur,' I said crisply, 'which I cannot discuss over the telephone. Could you call? Perhaps this afternoon?' It was as if someone else were speaking.

'That would be an honour, Madame.'

'You know my address, I think.'

'Shall we say . . . three o'clock?'

'Perfect.'

We said goodbye and I waited for the detective to call.

Henri Poincaret was as punctual as ever and I welcomed him myself into the sitting-room. He has the rolling gait of a prize-fighter and unfortunately short legs so it is hard to appreciate his special qualities. Though many take him for a fool – and he was, I believe, forced to leave Paris because of certain irregularities – I am reminded of a young and over-eager bloodhound who can always be trusted to catch a few rabbits, albeit the wrong ones.

For the third time that day I repeated the events surrounding my niece's disappearance. Poincaret asked a few questions without noting anything down so I was obliged to trust his memory. This time I gave him abbreviated biographies of all the people involved: of David Taverner and Claude in particular. He understood at once.

'You think,' he said crisply, 'that Monsieur . . . Taverner may have been involved?'

'It's perfectly possible. I say no more than that. I think it would be wise to see what he does next.'

'And Monsieur Cerda?'

'Monsieur Cerda is my friend. However . . .'

'I see.'

'Quite.'

I told him what Eveline had seen and gave him permission to question her further.

Poincaret left my house at 3.45 p.m. on the 25th of April. I had given him all the information he needed. Then I waited to see what would happen next.

11

THEY ALL crawled out of the woodwork one by one. I should have expected it. Father Thomas was first off the mark. He called early the next morning – a Saturday – brandishing a copy of *France-Antilles* which reported my niece's disappearance on the front page.

'My dear Madame,' said Father Thomas, pressing my hand zealously with his fat, pink palm, 'I think we should pray.'

'What, now?'

He clucked his tongue. 'God, in His infinite wisdom will provide . . .' It sounded as if Agnès had drawn a postal order on God's bounty which she might cash at any moment.

'I can't stay,' said Father Thomas, before I had asked him. 'My flock, you understand, they need me.' I nodded.

'But you'll be in church tomorrow morning?' he asked anxiously.

'I never fail.'

'We shall add our prayers to yours.'

More postal orders, I thought grimly. We have suffered a succession of Fathers, some born in these islands and others who arrive from France with misplaced missionary ideals: we are all Catholics here even if we confuse our saints with our spirits and worship them all despite unorthodox genealogies.

'And perhaps you would care to take tea with me this afternoon?'

I pictured his study with its flowered wallpaper, and the good woman who looks after him, and regretted I was already engaged. He shook my hand with such touching sincerity that I was ashamed of my ingratitude. I would make a point of speaking with him in church, after his prayers.

Next to arrive was Emile Leclerc, the curator with whom I conducted the long-standing argument over ownership of André's stones. As soon as I saw his tall, thin figure pick its way up the drive I guessed what he wanted and tried to disappear inside the house. He saw me and waved. I am not invisible. I felt forced to offer the man some refreshment but indicated to Eveline that the best china was unnecessary. He took his seat with the grace of a stick insect, all elbows and knees, and proceeded to stare over my head.

'I have heard,' he said, 'about your misfortune. Most distressing. You have my sympathies, Madame.'

'Thank you. Though I doubt if you came all this way to give me those.'

'Yes, I suppose you're right. My stones . . .'

'They are not *your* stones, Monsieur.'

'Forgive me, Madame. I anticipate . . . Let me start again. Your niece has vanished and according to the newspapers – though their information may be out-of-date – you have received no communication from the men who have taken her.'

'That is correct. I do not even know *if* she has been taken.'

'But she's not here.'

'Correct again.'

The curator, it seemed, had a plan – ingenious if a little fanciful. Leclerc assured me it would be a splendid gesture, one that would demonstrate beyond question that my heart was in the right place. He wanted me to announce – publicly – that I would exchange his blessed stones for the safe conduct of Agnès. Their gods for my niece. An unequal bargain, I thought.

'Monsieur,' I said, anxious to remove him from my sight, 'I think we should keep this affair in proportion. If I could be certain that such a gesture would save Agnès I would gladly comply. But we have no proof that anyone, apart from yourself, cares one whit for my stones. The position would of course be different if you yourself had some hand in her abduction . . . Indeed, I noted your absence from my party when Agnès was attacked.'

He left immediately. I had touched a raw nerve although I did not for a second consider him guilty of either offence. Nevertheless I thought it prudent to relay the conversation to Poincaret. In the event I told the story to his answering machine and said he should visit at the earliest opportunity.

Leclerc was followed by a clutch of journalists who asked the same questions, inspected my photograph album, took identical pictures of the house and forced me to revise my opinion of Taverner's professional competence. He was no worse than his peers.

Finally I told Eveline that I had suffered enough intrusions for one day and was no longer at home.

The waiting seemed interminable. I paced up and down my house. I telephoned Poincaret a second time and on being connected to his machine hung up immediately. My neighbours called, I think.

Madame de Ste Croix is absent.

There must be some mistake. We've seen her car.

I'm sorry. She's gone away.

To go walking in this heat? How strange. How very strange.

After my visitors had gone I slipped on to the veranda. The hours wore me down, each second counted, inspected, put aside. I felt forced against the wall, no longer mistress of my life. All I could do was wait while vultures circled overhead. At last I could bear it no longer and drove to the headland but saw at once Claude's house was locked and empty. On my way back I called in to see Achille Gonstran, first stopping on the bridge under which stagnant water reflected back the palm trees and pure, cloudless skies. Claude said this corner of the town reminded him of Indo-China; it is as beautiful and futile as our forgotten empire.

The Mayor was busy. As I had no appointment his secretary insisted that I take my turn like everyone else. Even kidnaps shall not disturb the smooth-running of our bureaucracy. So I sat on the hard wooden bench fanning myself with a newspaper, until he was free. Gonstran's room was in its habitual state of disorder. The man himself, in shirt sleeves, was buried under paperwork. As soon as he saw me he put on his jacket and rose to shake my hand. I swear he had tears in his eyes as he listened to my story which he had heard already from the newspapers and from the police. I told him about the Englishman, and the hiring of Poincaret, and Leclerc's mad suggestion.

'Madame,' he said when I had finished, 'I'm shocked by

what has happened but not surprised. No note, you said . . .'

'Not a word.'

'They keep silent even about their demands.'

'Perhaps they don't know what they want.'

'We've been friends for a long time. You trust me, I hope?'

I nodded. Gonstran was the only person, in fact, whom I trusted completely.

'I seem to recall hearing recently that your family wish you to return to France. And that is why your niece is visiting?'

'Yes, but my home is here.'

'No, Madame,' he said carefully, 'do not presume anything. Your home will never be here.'

'How dare you . . . This is France, after all.'

'Across the seas.'

'But *France*.'

Gonstran got to his feet and turned his back on me. 'You will all leave, sooner or later.'

'After my lifetime.'

'It can't go on for ever.'

I was conscious of the fan whirring overhead, and the mayor's unease. 'Take this as a warning,' he went on. 'There are forces at work which I don't fully understand.'

'You're meant to be in charge.'

'That too.'

'You have overstepped your brief, Monsieur. Like Leclerc you appear to expect some ridiculous gesture on my part. Give me my niece and I will leave the island . . . Is that your idea? I would become a laughing stock.'

'I'm not asking for a gesture, or a sacrifice. I'm thinking of your safety. There is another thing.'

'Yes, Monsieur?'

‘You should know what people are saying about you.’

‘I never listen to gossip.’

‘You will this time, Madame, for your own good. They are saying that you took Agnès yourself.’

I sat down heavily in my chair, unable to believe what I had heard.

Gonstran said, ‘There is one way to stop the rumours.’

‘And what is that?’

‘You must start legal proceedings immediately. Against the kidnappers.’

‘How can I, when I have no idea of their identity?’

‘Against persons unknown . . .’

Gonstran had taken leave of his senses. As if the completion of a form would halt their tongues or their imagination.

‘I won’t do it.’

‘Believe me, Madame, it’s the only way.’

‘We shall see,’ I said and left the room.

Reluctantly I crossed the square to the post office knowing I should notify Gustave and Marie-Louise of Agnès’s disappearance but what could I say? As it was late afternoon the room was crowded and I could barely think. In the end I wrote simply: AGNÈS GONE MISSING WILL WRITE REGARDS ALICIA, and fought my way to the head of the queue by pushing like the rest of them.

At my house, Poincaret was installed on the veranda looking well-pleased with himself. He had unearthed a rather vulgar straw hat, a shade too small, which thankfully he removed in my presence. The man had obviously exerted himself: his face was red and he had sweated unpleasantly under the armpits. He handed me the first of his reports which ran to several closely-typewritten pages. His skill with the typewriter was rudimentary, and he had not learnt to be brief. There was much ‘concealing of his person in the bushes', and each step of his deductions was recorded with childlike fidelity as if he sat an examination in which it is not the answer that counts but how one calculates the truth. For example, when David Taverner called on Claude, the latter was faithfully described – Caucasian male; height 1.70 m; age: 62 approx.; attire: tropical suit, light colour, no tie; colour of hair: grey – after which Poincaret commented, 'this answers to your description of Señor Claude Cerda, occupation poet, and I shall henceforth assume that it *was* Cerda, in the absence of proof to the contrary.'

At least I had no need to read between the lines. He told me everything: the exact time each action took place (except for a period of approximately two hours during which his watch had stopped), any notable features of the landscape, what was known about the people he followed and the status of that knowledge. I learnt, for instance, that Edouard Jouvé, who may have met Taverner the day after Agnès disappeared (identity unconfirmed) was leader of a group known as the *Santanistes*, loosely named after Ste Anne where Jouvé was born; that in spite of their title, the majority of the group came from Guadeloupe; that they were dedicated to Antillean independence; and that Jouvé had been suspected by the police of complicity in the recent Fort de France riots but owing to lack of evidence had been released with a stern warning from the authorities. I learnt also that Léopold Suvélor, unemployed carpenter, enjoyed a dubious reputation that included a scurrilous rumour of involvement with my family, and that the Caravelle peninsula, an area of outstanding natural beauty, had been designated a prime site of the island's *Parc Régional. Enfin.*

The principal events witnessed by my detective were as follows. Early on Saturday, the 26th of April, the day after Agnès's presumed kidnap, David Taverner was driven by Léopold to the lighthouse on the Caravelle where he met several young men. Poincaret, in the bushes, was too far away to catch their conversation. After this meeting Taverner returned briefly to his hotel and was then driven by Léopold (at alarming speed) to the house where Señor Cerda had taken up temporary residence. In the company of Cerda they had driven around the foothills of the mountain, stopping several times en route at wayside cafés. Each time Claude got out of the car (alone) and disappeared inside for a minute or two. He did not seem to be drinking. From this, Poincaret concluded that David Taverner was probably implicated in my niece's disappearance. First of all he consorted with unsavoury characters (Léopold) and suspected terrorists (the *Santanistes*, always assuming it was them). Second, Taverner looked guilty and, therefore, he was. I suggested tactfully that it might not be so simple. Claude on the other hand received only cursory attention from my detective, and I recommended that this be remedied at once as news of his random itinerary through the foothills was equally disturbing.

I asked Poincaret about the rumour that connected Léopold to my family. As I suspected, it concerned Angeline. For many years no one has mentioned her name and now she is on everyone's lips. The story goes that when Léopold was a young man, barely out of his teens, he had helped to get rid of her illegitimate daughter – not murdered, you understand, simply 'removed'. Poincaret swore the tale was without foundation and I let the matter pass.

I gave Poincaret permission to engage two additional assistants on the grounds that the case was 'exceedingly delicate' and 'running in several directions at once'. He also sought my assurance that all his expenses would be met including those for which he could not produce receipts. At Taverner's hotel he had been obliged to donate 50F to the barman, a sum that was wasted because while he made enquiries of the man, Taverner had descended the stairs. To extricate himself from any possible embarrassment Poincaret pretended the barman had misheard: he was not seeking a foreigner, *un étranger*, but someone who was rather odd, *étrange*, a point he demonstrated by pulling a variety of faces, puffing and blowing like a carthorse, so that the Englishman gave him a wide berth as they passed in the lobby. I said he must strive harder to maintain his anonymity which Poincaret interpreted as a slur on his professional reputation. It was, I suppose, in a way.

By the time we had reviewed all possible significances night had fallen. As he was leaving, Poincaret remembered the message on his answering machine, about Leclerc and his strange offer to exchange my stones for Agnès.

'Can I see them, Madame?' he asked.

'At this hour? They're outside in a clearing. And it's dark.'

'If you could accompany me.'

'I never go out to the plantation after the sun has set.'

'It might be important.'

'Oh very well. If you insist.'

I called Eveline who proposed her daughter, Yvette. While we waited for the child, I asked Poincaret what possible significance Leclerc and his mad suggestion could have in the disappearance of Agnès. I remember he said that we should leave no stone unturned.

Yvette arrived and stared at us in her sulky fashion. Her hair was matted and unclean and she looked even more of a savage than usual. Poincaret fetched a torch from his car and the two set off in the darkness. I wondered if I had hired the right man to solve my mysteries.

The detective returned within an hour, alone. He was out of breath and looked as if he had seen a ghost. He told me that the stones had gone.

'What do you mean, gone?'

'They are not there, Madame . . .'

'Are you sure you looked in the right place?'

'The girl seemed certain of it . . . And there were signs of disturbance. We found a broken pickaxe and a number of sacks.'

'I cannot tolerate such carelessness. First I lose Agnès, and now the stones which have belonged to my husband's family for more than three hundred years.'

Poincaret looked crestfallen, as if he had mislaid them himself. He asked for a full description of the stones and promised to look into the matter. Then he left, not before time.

That night I had dinner alone, watching the shadows from my candles flicker against the wall. Outside the wind quickened and the rain came swiftly. After it had moved up the valley I telephoned Claude who was not at home. Like Agnès I felt that they had all deserted me.

The next day, Sunday, I went to Mass as soon as the bells called. Madame Dassein from the post office spoke to me gently as we went up the steps, and others came to shake my hand: Pierre and Suzanne d'Aurigny, with Olivier; Madeleine who keeps the general store; Monsieur Farrugia, the postman; Victor from the bank with his sons; all the good people among whom I live out my days. A handshake, the eyes averted, a stammered, '*Condoléances, Madame.*'

For most of the service I stared out of shuttered windows to the bright glare beyond, and traced the image of coloured glass above the shutters. The choir sounded unusually exquisite and even Father Thomas's prayers were good. We prayed for the safe return of Agnès Montfort who, in the short time she had dwelt among us, had touched our hearts with her simplicity.

Agneau de Dieu, qui effacez les péchés du monde, pardonnez-nous, Jésus. Agneau de Dieu, qui effacez les péchés du monde, exaucez-nous, Jésus. Agneau de Dieu, qui effacez les péchés du monde, ayez pitié de nous, Jésus. Jésus, écoutez-nous. Jésus, exaucez-nous.

Father Thomas neglected to point out that on two Sundays out of five Agnès had failed to appear in church. At times like these it is right to show a little charity. After I had acknowledged his words of sympathy on the steps of the church – and declined a second invitation to tea – I walked up the headland to the statue of Our Lady where several parked cars disturbed my meditations. I did not continue to Claude's. As I walked slowly back to the square I passed a group of boys sitting on the wall by the monsoon drain. Their surly glances and sharp mocking laughter were obviously produced for my benefit. They repeated the rumour about what I might have done with Agnès.

That afternoon I composed my letter to Gustave. It was one of the most difficult I have ever written, harder even than those brief expressions of regret when family and friends pass on. I wished neither to cause my brother alarm, nor to absolve him entirely from his share of blame. It was several hours before I was satisfied, and the floor around my bureau was littered with the evidence of false beginnings.

Plantation Ste Croix
St Antoine
Martinique

Sunday, 27 April

Dear Gustave,
You will have received my telegram by now so I shall get straight to the point. Your daughter Agnès has disappeared. The police – and most of the others on this island – assume she has been kidnapped, and I am assured that every effort is being made to track her down. They have set up road blocks in the hills and rounded up various unsavoury characters for questioning. I think this affair will result in the resolution of a number of other mysteries, in addition to the identity of her abductors.

I am certain that Agnès will come to no harm and that she will shortly rejoin us, making light of her adventures. Do not ask me how I am so certain: just trust me, Gustave, and my optimism. I think it wise, however, that as soon as she returns she should leave these islands forthwith. One does not tempt providence more often than is absolutely necessary. She is a headstrong girl and has been mixing with the wrong kind of people. I say no more than that but take note that I have my evidence.

You may criticise me for not controlling her more firmly, to which I plead guilty, abominably guilty, but she is your daughter and arrived with the manners of her upbringing. The Church teaches that our children reach the age of reason at seven. Even at twenty-one, Agnès's development must be regarded as suspect. I hope I have made myself clear.

I told you that I had no intention of leaving the island. In direct contradiction of my wishes you sent me your beloved daughter to entice me back to your fold. I have asked you already to take her away. Now she has vanished and we should recognise in her disappearance a warning to us all. Once we have found Agnès you must leave me in peace.

Please convey my regards and sympathies to Marie-Louise.

Your loving sister,
Alicia.

After I had completed the letter, time began to weigh heavily, and I spent some moments in André's study contemplating his maps whose every landmark was imprinted on my soul. It was Eveline's day off and she had gone to visit her family at Rivière Pilote. I longed for company, for the sound of cheerful laughter, and would even have welcomed the sight of Yvette slinking across the lawn.

Three hours before sunset one of Poincaret's assistants arrived with two sealed envelopes for my attention. The fellow, a young mulatto – almost white-skinned – introduced himself as Max. I did not catch his surname. Poincaret himself had departed that morning for Fort de France and had not been heard of since.

I told Max to wait in the car while I read the reports. Both were handwritten by the detectives and reasonably presented. The first concerned David Taverner. Max had taken up position outside the Hôtel des Innocents in the early hours of Sunday morning. Taverner was at his window and the clicking of his typewriter echoed down the empty street. It appears he had been writing all night. Max had bribed a chambermaid who managed to secure a page of Taverner's efforts. Though written in English, and lacking both a beginning and an end, it provided clear proof of his stupidity as he had not only developed a philosophical defence of terrorism, but had stated categorically that the kidnapping of Agnès Montfort was one step on the road to a more just society. The man disappointed me. I had expected more of him than muddled platitudes about ends and means. I put the paper aside. It had been produced on a French typewriter with which Taverner was obviously unfamiliar and the English letters were sprinkled unhelpfully with our accents.

I turned to the second envelope which contained a much shorter report on Claude. He, too, had been writing at his window though with none of the Englishman's frenzy. He had spent most of the morning staring out to sea in a state of complete immobility. I wondered what he thought of – whether he remembered Agnès, for example, or me, or whether his stillness was evidence of the creative mind at work.

Around midday he had started to write, on one sheet of paper only. The other assistant, Jacques, displayed his ingenuity by persuading some fishermen to create a disturbance along the beach in return for a couple of bottles of rum. One of them shouted for help so loudly that Claude left the house to see what was going on. Jacques, meanwhile, who had been hiding round the back of the bungalow, nipped smartly inside intending to memorise what Claude had written. He had forgotten it would be in Spanish. He managed to write down the title then heard the sound of Claude's footsteps on the wooden stairs and was forced to jump out of a window. Claude had written a poem, a very short poem without any corrections, which he had called *Señora de la noce*. It was possibly a final draft.

I considered my evidence. I had Agnès's diary. I had the first of Poincaret's reports and those of his assistants. I had a piece of paper that belonged to David Taverner and the knowledge that Claude had transcribed a short poem entitled 'Lady of the Night'. I no longer had my stones. The trouble was that none of it fitted together. Did Taverner, for instance, believe what he had written about my niece's kidnap? What was Claude seeking in the foothills? And who on earth had stolen André's stones?

Monsieur Cerda says that when people die they go to the city of angels. El pueblo de los angeles. It sounds better in Spanish don't you think, Aunt Lily?

Only André dared to call me Lily.

I knew then what I should do. I went outside and instructed Max that he should take David Taverner's paper at once to Mayor Gonstran, who could ably judge its significance. Until such time as the Mayor might respond, Max should continue to keep Taverner under surveillance. Jacques should continue likewise with Claude. As for Poincaret, I revealed my displeasure that he should delegate all his responsibilities to subordinates.

I knew also it was imperative I found out what Claude had written. Aware that Poincaret was not the man for literary conversations, I would have to call myself if I wished to get closer to the truth.

12

MY MOTIVE in sending Max to the Mayor with Taverner's defence of terrorism was to teach the man a lesson, namely that he should keep out of the affairs of others. Hindsight dictates I should have confronted Taverner with the evidence myself, thus safeguarding us from the consequences of his actions. It is, of course, easy to be wise. Afterwards.

We do not know how Taverner spent the 25th of April after he left my house. I picture him at his room in that cheap hotel, staring down at the street and the futile arrogance of the sea. Vauclin is a cold and windy place full of skinny dogs and barefoot, ragged children. As Agnès said, it is the end of the road.

Early on the morning of the 26th of April, Léopold called at the hotel and the pair set out to a meeting with Edouard

Jouvé and the *Santanistes*, as Poincaret had correctly surmised. This may have been arranged by Taverner himself. Agnès, you will recall, noted a prior meeting between Taverner and the *Santanistes* on the 5th. They drove through Tartane at 140 kilometres an hour, my unnerved detective sticking grimly to their tail. Before the ruins of the Château Dubuc the metalled road ends and a dirt track, closed to motor vehicles, continues to the lighthouse. Ignoring the road signs, Léopold took the Peugeot along the track while my detective, a more law-abiding citizen, followed on foot, aided by the rutted surface of the road which restricted Léopold to an unnatural crawl. Jouvé and his gang waited for Taverner in a corrugated iron shed below the lighthouse. Poincaret settled himself in the bushes and watched the group through binoculars.

Jouvé told Taverner that they held Agnès Montfort a prisoner. They were prepared to release her on the following condition: that David Taverner (whom they had mistaken for a foreign correspondent of international repute) should pen a strongly-worded article extolling their virtues and justifying their actions. He was, in other words, to represent their point of view.

Poincaret notes that this conversation took thirty-three minutes. It is unlikely, therefore, that Taverner agreed at once to their demands. First, he had no proof that they had captured Agnès and second, his dented reputation was at stake. His newspaper's editorial policy was not so catholic as to sanction glowing profiles of every hare-brained dreamer who brandishes a gun in the name of justice and freedom. But the Englishman had decided, rather late in the day, that he had fallen in love with my niece and he prized her life more highly than his professional reputation. He agreed to consider their demands and was allowed to return to his hotel, my detective still on his heels. (Though only just:

Poincaret lost Léopold after Tartane and fortunately was able to deduce their likely destination.)

Taverner was warned by the *Santanistes* that the girl would be shot if he approached the police or Agnès's family. This gave him an unexpected loophole. From Vauclin he telephoned Claude for advice because he could not seriously believe either that the *Santanistes* had captured Agnès; or – if they had taken her – that they might harm her. In his previous meetings he had classed them as dreamers, fuelled by hope and hot air. Claude was more inclined to take them at their word, remembering his moonlit encounter with Hector, that wild young man, who had given warning of a kidnap. Perhaps Hector was one of the *Santanistes*.

At Claude's suggestion the two men set out on their abortive search in mountain cafés, with Léopold and his friend Gaspard who joined them for the ride. Hector had no distinguishing features apart from his name (which may have been assumed), and a missing front tooth, so it is hardly surprising that no information was forthcoming.

Taverner felt he had no choice. Bolstered with cheap whisky he spent a long night complying with Jouvé's demands. The next morning, a chambermaid who had been bribed by Max knocked at the door and asked to make his bed. As he had not slept in it he sent her away. With a second bribe the girl strode boldly into the bedroom and said she really must tidy up. Taverner left. She stole one of the papers from a pile on his desk, and made a half-hearted attempt to clean the room. After she had gone the Englishman spent another hour or so on his article, then placed a collect call to London. The incredulous sub-editor, to whom he read his story, pointed out that Taverner's argument was full of holes. (Both men were ignorant that one of the more crucial pages was missing. Taverner had, after all, passed a sleepless night.) The sub-editor said he would need to clear the story and that in his view it would be rejected. Taverner maintained it was 'important'. He drank more whisky (it was now 10 a.m.) and went to bed fully dressed after telling the manager he must not be disturbed, even by a call from London. If they did not print the story there was nothing more he could do.

Taverner was woken in the late afternoon by a man with dark glasses, a beret and a conspicuous limp, who said that Achille Gonstran wanted to see him at the *mairie*. When he protested it was Sunday, the man quickly became aggressive. Taverner put on a clean shirt, dusted down his badly-creased trousers, and was driven up the coast to St Antoine.

Gonstran himself unlocked the door to the *mairie* and showed Taverner into his upstairs office. The rest of the building was empty, except for the man with the limp who stood guard outside in the street. Gonstran sat behind his desk under the desultory fan which breathed a semblance of life into his papers. The bells rang for vespers and figures could be seen ambling across the square to the church. The town seemed peaceful enough.

'Passport,' said the mayor suddenly after he and Taverner had played their game of cat and mouse with more conventional exchanges.

Taverner handed over his papers. He had entered the Union of Soviet Socialist Republics at Kaliningrad and flown out from Moscva. He had been in the Seychelles for the mutiny and Paris for the recent bombings. A frequent visitor to the Lebanon and the Hashemite Kingdom of Jordan he had also visited the Oman, the People's Democratic Republic of Yemen, the United Arab Emirates and parts of Africa including Benin, the Central African Empire, Gabon, Burundi, Rwanda, and Upper Volta. The mayor studied the document with care. At last he lay it on the desk and stared with renewed interest at the Englishman who looked tired but otherwise relaxed.

'Do you smoke?'

Taverner shook his head.

'No?' Gonstran picked up the passport and said icily, 'You do not appear to have entered the island, Monsieur. Can you explain this omission or am I talking to a ghost?'

Taverner took the passport and, like the mayor, tracked his journeys through the stamps of tiny kingdoms and improbable republics.

'You're quite right,' he said. 'How curious. I don't seem to be here.'

'I could have you deported.'

'I think that would be unwise . . .'

'You're threatening me?'

'I'm not in such a fortunate position, Monsieur. But my paper . . .'

'To hell with your newspaper. I'm talking about you and what brings you to Martinique.'

'I'm a foreign correspondent – it says so in my passport.'

'I can read as well as you. However, I do not necessarily accept such statements at face value. You enter the country illegally . . .'

'I was offered a lift.'

'Shut up. I know it for a fact. You stay here two, three weeks, maybe more, and from what I know of your movements you care little for our sights.'

'I have travelled a lot since I arrived.'

'Exactly. And to the wrong places.'

'You have had me followed?'

'Let's say I trust in the efficacy of spot checks.'

'Perhaps I'm on holiday?' suggested Taverner hopefully.

'Don't take me for a fool. What are you doing here?'

Taverner did not answer. Since their first meeting at my

party he had run across Gonstran occasionally in St Antoine and once in Le Robert, all cordial encounters at which the Mayor had reminded him of his advice that he should not write about flowers. It had become quite a joke between them: 'Keeping off the flowers?' Gonstran would say before slapping Taverner on the back. This meeting was different, however, and Gonstran appeared to have forgotten his earlier camaraderie.

The Mayor removed from his desk drawer a sheet of paper which Taverner did not immediately recognise, and laid it between them on the desk after sweeping his documents to one side, some of which fell off the edge of his desk together with a basket of correspondence. He put on a pair of gold-rimmed spectacles and translating slowly (and badly) said, 'Can you explain what you meant when you wrote that the taking of Agnès Montfort is one step on the road to a more just society in which the dispossessed shall regain title to their lands and the key to their houses?'

'Not houses – heritage,' said Taverner, then stopped. He wanted to tear the paper from Achille Gonstran's hands.

'So it was you,' murmured Gonstran. 'I must presume also it was you who wrote . . . what does it say . . . "No one is innocent," by which I assume you refer to the Montfort girl?'

The Mayor pushed away the paper in disgust. 'What have you done with her?'

'What have I done . . . ?' Taverner stared at him helplessly, '. . . with Agnès?'

'Where is she?'

'You don't understand.'

'You have made your position absolutely clear,' said Gonstran, indicating the paper.

'Oh that . . . It's all lies, utter nonsense.'

'Many take it for the truth.'

'They have a point, Monsieur. They have been badly treated.'

'Who, exactly, are "they"?'

The two men stared at each other.

Taverner said, 'You must believe me, sir. I've done nothing with Agnès. I don't know where she is. That . . . paper . . . What I wrote was designed to bring her back.'

'It has magical properties?' Gonstran enquired holding up the offending page as if it might bite him. He leaned forward across his desk, toying with a pencil in his large black hands. 'I would be interested to know what you have learned since you arrived.'

'Well,' said Taverner, uncertainly, 'you have your . . . problems, like everyone else.'

'*Problems*? We need a foreign correspondent to tell us we have problems?' The pencil broke in his hands and he tossed the pieces into the waste paper basket.

'Yes,' said Taverner. 'The unemployment rate is . . . er, increasing . . . I understand that a considerable proportion of the population is dissatisfied with the level of family allowances . . . Then there's education. The left-wing intelligentsia is over-educated for the opportunities that exist on the island . . .' He sounded as if he read from a notebook. The Mayor stood up abruptly and strode across to the window. Outside darkness was falling rapidly.

'Come here,' he ordered. Taverner jumped to his feet.

'Out there is our problem,' said the Mayor, taking hold of Taverner's arm. 'Not the unemployment rate or a little squabble over family allowances. Out there, the silence . . .'

Taverner tried to disengage himself from Gonstran's grip.

'Can't you hear it?' He was shouting, holding the Englishman even more tightly. 'Out there, listen.'

Taverner tried to wriggle free.

'We speak to be silent . . . We sing songs to be silent.'

'Look, I'm sorry.'

'Shut up! Oh yes, we're well educated in the banalities of Marxist-Leninism. What the hell do they know of our predicament? And all your damned libertarians. Man is born free and is everywhere in chains . . . Was *his* great grandfather a slave? Was *he* beaten and starved and treated like shit, worse than shit, to give him the right to speak for us? *Listen to the silence*, and then you may understand why we have problems.'

He shook Taverner roughly, like a chicken. A motorbike revved in the square below. In the distance a dog barked, followed by another. The man with a limp, standing guard at the door, said very clearly, 'The Mayor is occupied right now, you cannot see him.'

Taverner looked at Gonstran and shook his head. There was no silence.

Gonstran let go of his arm and walked dejectedly back to his desk. The other man remained at the window, peering out at small figures who emerged from the church in the gathering gloom.

'Let me explain something,' said Gonstran staring at his hands. 'I have a son, a doctor, who studied in Paris. He came back to a good job at the hospital and we respect him, all of us. He's a good son, a good husband, a good doctor, and he'll soon be a good father. But he's decided to leave, to throw everything up and go away.'

'I don't see . . .'

'He says he can't cure his own sickness. So he will go away, to regain his hope. For my part . . .' The man shrugged. 'I am a pessimist. I grow a little older, that's all.'

'I'm sorry,' mumbled Taverner.

'Don't mention it. Now tell me what you did with Agnès.'

The Mayor is a clever man. I was right to think that he alone could sap Taverner's stubborn resistance. Perhaps he had already guessed the other's weak spot because when Taverner continued to assert his ignorance, Gonstran produced the first of the posters of Agnès which were to become such an obsessive feature of our landscape. I found them disconcerting, to say the least. It is unpleasant to encounter one's missing relatives whenever one turns a corner. Many of these posters disappeared. She was, by common consent, a pretty girl.

Taverner was especially pained by the sight of Agnès smiling at him over her shoulder, enveloped by the warm ocean winds: he had taken the photograph himself near Ste Anne and though distorted by the enlargement, the image caught her insouciant good looks and the vagaries of her smile. Gonstran switched on the light over his desk and left Taverner alone with Agnès.

When Gonstran returned after thirty minutes, the Englishman related in a monotone how he had met Jouvé who claimed to have kidnapped Agnès and wished to bargain for her release. To be fair, Taverner did not immediately reveal Jouvé's name but Agnès's life was at stake and Gonstran insisted that the girl could not be found if the kidnappers remained anonymous. The Mayor was curious to know what proof Jouvé had given to show that his group had taken Agnès.

'He gave me his word.'

'We're a race of opportunists.'

'I had to believe him. I had no choice.'

Gonstran telephoned the Commissaire de Police in Fort de France and relayed this information without implicating Taverner. Such a gesture is typical of a man who seeks to preserve the self-respect of others. Taverner was obliged to remain at the *mairie* in case his conscience rebelled and prompted him to alert the *Santanistes*. He waited for news in Gonstran's office where they were joined by the man with the limp. Conversation was minimal.

When the telephone rang at about 11 p.m., all three started. Gonstran picked up the receiver and listened to the Commissaire who informed him that the exercise had been successful. Jouvé's haunts were well-known and the chief members of the gang had been rounded up in a bar in Fort de France, plus one or two stragglers taken from their beds. Everything had gone according to plan with one exception: they had not found a single trace of Agnès.

13

MONDAY THE 28th of April. I knew nothing of the business with Jouvé. I rose early with the dawn to prepare for my visit to Claude, on whom my happiness depended. He should have flowers as he did the day he came, red flowers from the garden I tend as a bulwark against the rank putrescence of the jungle. The clouds swooped low over the water, and Pelée to the north was invisible. I shivered in the early morning air. The sight which greeted me was distressing. Several hibiscus had sprouted cancroid growths; they should be uprooted and burnt without delay and I would miss them, I thought, for a time. Contemplating the ruin of my garden I did not hear the footsteps behind me. A hand pressed on my shoulder. I swung round, dropping my flowers, my secateurs, my basket. It was Henri Poincaret in shorts. He apologised profusely for the shock he had given me and stooped to retrieve my possessions. As well as the shorts he wore a striped shirt, tennis shoes and long white socks, possibly as a form of disguise. I asked what he wanted at such an early hour – the sun had barely risen above the trees. He announced portentously that he had found my stones. I remarked that actually I had hired him to find my niece.

'That's the point, Madame. They've given me an idea.'

'Like our friend Monsieur Taverner?'

'I beg your pardon?'

'He entertains ideas too, and look where they get us.'

'Quite so, Madame.'

I regarded him closely to see if he mocked me. With Poincaret it is impossible to guess. He is a small man, no taller than I, and was looking so inflated with his ideas I feared he might burst. I enquired reluctantly about my stones, knowing he would pester me until I had done so. The previous day, guided by an unaccustomed presentiment, he had visited Leclerc's museum in Fort de France where at closing time he had hidden behind a cabinet full of glass-eyed marmosets, black rats, a salamander, and the deadly *fer de lance*. I told him to get on with the story unless such natural history was in any way relevant (it was not). The museum was empty apart from the shadows of stuffed animals and my detective who groped his way around the show cases, looked in corners, stumbled up the stairs, down the stairs, until at last he came to Leclerc's office in the basement. (The man's name was written on the door. That point, at least, was relevant.)

'Well,' said Poincaret, mopping his brow with a handkerchief, 'what do you think?'

'I haven't the faintest idea. *You* are the detective, Monsieur.'

'The stones, Madame. That's what I found.'

He positively glowed with pleasure. The stones, still in

their sacks, lay in a corner of Leclerc's office. The man was clearly a thief. I told him for the last time that I did not care about the stones: they were part of my heritage but as nothing compared with my brother's child. As soon as he had recognised that simple fact we might do business together. I snapped at my bushes with the secateurs. Poincaret deflated before my eyes, as if he had expected a medal and been court-martialled for his pains. He glanced at his feet and tucked his shirt into his shorts. Prompted by concern for the fellow's dignity I thought it kindest to enquire after the nature of his other 'ideas'. Sulking, he said he would inform me later, in his reports, if they matured. And was it true that André had collected maps?

'I don't see what my late husband . , .'

'Old maps. Of the island?'

'That is so.'

'And of the estate?'

'Several. Very valuable ones. They're out of date of course because much of the land has been sold. They hang in his study.'

'If you would be so kind, Madame, I should like to consult them.'

'Are you lost?'

'By no means, Madame. I merely wish to see them.'

I made it plain that I considered his request eccentric. If he could not afford to purchase maps himself they could be obtained, on my account, from Madeleine's store in the town.

Poincaret stuck to his purpose. Only André's maps would suffice. It was simplest to humour him. Eveline met us at the top of the steps. When she saw the white man in shorts she clapped her hands and burst into good-natured laughter. Poincaret ignored her. I asked her to take him into the study and show him the maps on the wall. He was to have every assistance. She led him away, laughing and speaking patois to him like a child.

Before I had finished my breakfast a police car drew up. It seemed that with Agnès gone, the comings and goings of the world were determined to wash up on the doorstep of my quiet home in the valley. A young captain showed me a series of photographs, all men in their early twenties, black men and brown men with hostile features and a mad defiance in their eyes. We lay the photographs before us as if for solitaire. Though he did not say so, these were the *Santanistes*, a motley crew of hotheads and petty criminals who hardly merited the term of bandit. Had I seen any of their fraternity lurking around the house? In the plantation perhaps? Were they friends of Agnès? Did I recognise them myself? I shook my head; they were not the kind of men to encourage on my lands. We called Eveline who was the sole witness to Agnès's disappearance. She studied each photograph with the utmost concentration. At last she also shook her head. Instinct told her these were not the men who had taken Agnès away. The captain, plainly disappointed, questioned her closely. She dramatised her story with several extraneous details. In this new version, she caught a glimpse of the fellows' faces and they had lost their hats. I took the captain aside and suggested that he consult Eveline's original statement to avoid chasing after hares. He left, saying we should contact him if we noticed anything suspicious.

Pépé brought the newspaper that had been delivered to the bottom of the steps. A short item in the stop press announced further developments in the Agnès Montfort affair. Following the receipt of secret information, several men were helping the police with their enquiries. I assumed this meant Jouvé, and said a silent prayer for the efforts of my friend the mayor. Pépé wanted his instructions. I told him of the cancer in my bushes, which should be destroyed immediately. He asked for kerosene, and an axe.

As I left the house, Poincaret emerged from the study holding a notebook which he had covered with drawings as infantile as the faces on my stones. He had quite slipped my mind. We said good day to each other, rather coldly, then he set off up the track that leads past the mango trees into the plantation, carrying a hat in anticipation of the sun.

In St Antoine I posted express the letter I had written to Gustave. When re-crossing the square a car veered around the corner and headed straight towards me. It missed me by centimetres. The driver stuck his head out of the window and shouted a coarse insult before thundering out of sight. He left behind an angry echo in the sun-bleached square.

Claude sat at his desk before the open window, exactly as described by Jacques, Poincaret's assistant. He neither moved nor wrote and gave no indication that he had seen me as I walked across the sands, though he stared at me glassily with the impenetrable eyes of the blind. I had never visited him before in the mornings (the time devoted to his work), and my nerve faltered – I could disappear behind the trees and he might think that he had only dreamt me. Too late. He raised one hand in greeting and I gathered my fragile courage like a cloak.

We sat on either side of the table in his cell-like room, before us a sheaf of paper and a selection of pens. I had forgotten my flowers.

It is extraordinarily difficult to talk to a person who is absent. Absent in mind, that is, not body: now that André is gone I tell him everything. But Claude . . . He sat beside me and we talked and I cannot call it a conversation. I asked him about ends and means. Perhaps he thought I referred to politics, or to Taverner's recent dilemma, because he spoke of his godson who planted bombs in Chilean cafés frequented by the wives and children of the *junta*. They found his body one morning in a ditch, charred and mutilated almost beyond recognition. Nails ripped from flesh. His once-handsome face scorched with the pock marks of burns. Blood dried black in the sun. An unremarked and unremarkable Christ in the gutter who died for an idea without the adulation of millions to show for it.

'Was he right to fight for the liberation of his country?'

'Of course,' I replied, 'if he believed in it enough.'

'And those who tortured him? They believed just as passionately in their cause. Their wives and children were slaughtered like beasts in an abattoir. Were they right too?'

'Why do you ask me this? You know I can't answer.'

'Camus,' he said, 'you've heard of him?'

'Of course.' (I am French, after all.)

' "I believe in justice but I will defend my mother before justice . . ." Do you understand what he meant? Do you?'

I held up my hands for him to stop. The trouble with parables is that they are never directly applicable to one's more mundane experience. My battle lines were not so starkly drawn. I asked what troubled him. Claude laughed bitterly. He was an intellectual. He had fought for ideas and kept his hands clean. He was disgusted with the contradictions in his life. And freedom? He cared for freedom more than anything in the world but knew that the greatest evil stems from the belief that you are right; that no matter what you do your God is with you. He turned towards me. He talked to himself and I happened to overhear.

'There must always be room,' he said, 'for reasonable doubt.'

Claude is the bravest man I have ever known: he denied himself the comfort of certitude.

I could not bear his talk of death and mutilation, his private Calvaries, with Agnès gone and life a sadder thing. I had not come for this. Beyond the palm trees bursts of sunlight flashed at intervals like code. Perhaps Poincaret's assistant stalked us through binoculars. I went to the window. A small dark shape lurked among the fishermen's nets hanging to dry in the sun. Claude sat at the table, his back towards me. I longed for our other conversations, about reflections of light on the water, about my late husband and Claude's daughters, conversations to which I could usefully contribute. I have nothing whatever to say on the morality of torture. I moved to his side. Claude reached for my hand and I felt immeasurably stronger than he, aware of my force flowing into his veins. Then I asked what would happen to Agnès.

'I'm frightened for her,' I said, 'she's just a child.'

'No, Alicia, a woman. A very beautiful woman.'

'I love her you know, but I hate her too. Why is that?'

'Because she is you.'

'What do you mean?'

'We see ourselves in others every day. And you're jealous of her.'

'Have I cause to be jealous?'

'She is so young . . .'

'And pretty. You said so yourself.'

'Perhaps. That's not what I meant. She has everything ahead of her.'

'While I have only my memories.'

'We grow older, you and I.'

'She will displace me?'

'It is inevitable.'

'There is something I must ask you.'

'Don't, Alicia, I warn you. There is nothing you *must* ask.'

'But Agnès . . .'

'Forget her. She ties us in knots.'

'Is it wrong to want to know?'

'Yes. Knowledge is not the same as understanding. We can know something for a fact and it doesn't help at all.'

'I read her diary, you know.'

Claude watched me. I felt his eyes upon my face, boring downwards until he reached my soul. I forgot to breathe. That minute stretched to eternity. What was it Agnès said? *I walk a tightrope high above the world and cannot possibly fall . . .* The moment passed. I returned somewhat rudely to earth. Claude watched me and smiled and was no longer absent. He had taken me with him as he would do always (and as he has done even now when he is far away in Durango). We laughed, I think, and Claude said happily that a man should live in his own country. I told him André would surely approve. He said his house was finished and lacked only the sounds of habitation, the laughter of his daughters and their friends. (We neither of us mentioned the generals.)

We left the house and walked towards the rocks, past the fishermen who loitered near their boats, and when we faced the Ilet St Aubin Claude took my hand and confessed to the imminent arrival aboard a yacht of his little girls, Isabella and Rosa. The prospect of more visitors disturbing the habits of our peaceful ways frightened me so much I could not immediately share my friend's enthusiasm.

I heard a noise behind us, and thought I saw a face among the scrub.

Claude said, 'You will love my daughters as I do.'

'They have a yacht?' I asked, striving to overcome my forebodings.

'No Alicia. I should not have told you. I should take better care of my secrets. The yacht belongs to my friends. They're very rich. I'm rich too but they are more so.'

'When are they expected?'

'Tomorrow, perhaps, or the day after, depending on the tides.'

So soon. More scufflings from the rocks behind us. A car backfired up on the headland and below us a fisherman began to dance on the sands, sweeping out his arms. Claude clapped his appreciation and turning to me explained it was the dance of his homeland, the *cueca*, which he had taught the men one drunken night in a bar. The fisherman looked up at us and waved. My friend kicked his heels on the rocks. His mercurial moods confused me: first his godson, then Agnès, and now this peasant joy which irradiated his features. He stopped suddenly and said he wished to recite a poem which owed its inspiration to me, because I preserved strange rhythms of other centuries when we had time for stillness and believed in grace. Before I could say that I wished to hear this more than anything in the world he stood before me and declaimed his love in a language I did not understand but which spoke from the heart, and I was touched by the canorous rhymes and his expression of awe, knowing that for once he was truly frightened by his gift which he laid at my feet as one would a wounded bird. No man could give me more.

We walked to the end of the beach. He held my arm close to his body and I felt the strength of his step and the pride of his bearing. After saying goodbye I drove along the road to my house, every inch of which I know by heart, past the sugar cane bending in the wind, the shacks and shanty towns of the workforce, the secondary jungle that creeps back at the earliest opportunity, and I hoped for the future.

The iron gates to the estate were open, in contradiction of my orders. Blaming Pépé, I resolved to be rid of him. As if by telepathy the fellow jumped from the bushes wielding an axe and shouting incoherently. I braked in time to avoid running him over. He clutched at the door and gabbled something about Agnès. Ordering him out of the way I accelerated up the drive in response to a growing fear that something terrible had happened.

I rounded the final corner. A car was parked by the steps. Next to it Poincaret sprawled on the grass, motionless and bloodied (though he still lived). A slogan had been painted on my walls, one we could not ignore. Red paint. *Black vengeance. White death.* From the house came repeated shrieks and the crashing of furniture. Five men emerged at the top of the steps. Two held Agnès by the arms. She would not go gently with them, but kicked and screamed and tried to pull away. A third man, Edouard Jouvé, held a gun to her back. I recognised Taverner's pistol. Pépé ran behind me up the drive, waving his axe. I stopped the car violently and felt him run into the back. Agnès saw me and cried for help. My mind went numb. I should have told her that the pistol was unloaded. The men dragged her down the steps and pushed her roughly into the car which sprang to life, my niece screaming all the while to me and to Poincaret who sat up, head in hands. I re-started the engine and we drove towards each other from opposite directions, gathering speed, grimly. At the last moment they swerved across the lawn, digging up the turf, and headed towards the gate, Agnès pinioned on the back seat, a victim, innocent, her terrified cries growing fainter as they skidded into the gateposts with the dull crash of bodywork on iron, the driver battling with the wheel. He gained control, turned northwards, and disappeared.

It was several seconds before I realised that what I had witnessed was the real taking of Agnès.

14

LOUD MOANS from Poincaret. His lips were cut and bled profusely; one eye so badly swollen I feared for his sight. With the aid of Eveline's uncle I dragged his body across the gravel and sat him against the side of the house down which the red paint dripped in rivulets, glinting in the sun. *Vengeance noire. Mort blanche.* A manifest warning. A woman's death. Poincaret sank to the ground. Cradling his head in my arms I got rid of Pépé who sprinted out of sight, muttering Hail Marys to himself. When we were alone I asked Poincaret to recount what had happened. He opened one eye and staring up at me stammered painfully, 'I f-f-found her . . .'

'So I see.'

'B-b-but . . . they . . . took her.'

'Jouvé and the *Santanistes*?'

He nodded in my arms.

'Where did you find her?' I asked coldly.

He groaned.

'My niece,' I persisted. 'Agnès Montfort. Where was she?'

He shook his head like a dog, spattering my hands with blood.

'The hurri . . . hu . . . hurricane . . . shelter,' he gasped with titanic effort.

Henri Poincaret had achieved the impossible. He had stumbled across Agnès's hiding place, which had eluded the island's entire police force. She who was lost is found and gone for ever. I wanted to strike him dead.

We stitched together his story, Poincaret retching for breath as I tried to staunch the blood from his wounds. Leclerc's theft of the stones had indeed given him an idea: if the stones were found in the one place they belonged – a museum dedicated to the island's history – perhaps the same logic might apply to the mystery of Agnès. The girl belonged with me which explained why Poincaret had wished to consult André's maps. They had revealed the existence of a number of possible hiding places including a Hindu temple, a ruined rum distillery, and the hurricane shelter near the northern borders on land now leased to the Compagnie Générale d'Outre Mer. He had visited all three and found Agnès locked in the shelter, having first to break down the door. The girl was strangely calm, sitting upright on a rough wooden bed surrounded by blankets. Poincaret was most insistent that in spite of her captivity she looked reasonably well cared for and had been fed at regular intervals. (I said a silent prayer for that, at least.) She had passed the time singing and repeating to herself a number of stories. She also said she was sorry for the trouble she had caused, and Poincaret wondered if she had cracked under the strain. He led her back to the house. As they mounted the steps, Agnès leaning on his arm, a car had driven up and five men jumped out. Edouard Jouvé. Hervé Gounel. Félix Lépine. Pascal Fontenaist. A man called Hector. After a moment's hesitation they swarmed up the steps and chased Agnès to her room from which she emerged screaming and waving Taverner's gun. She was swiftly disarmed. Poincaret was beaten down the steps, a slogan painted on the wall, my niece abducted.

When Eveline returned she found me crouched beside the supine body of my detective, his head in my lap, his blood swirled in abstract patterns on my dress. She regarded us with horror and went into the house. Hearing her cries of distress I laid Poincaret's head on the ground and followed her inside. The room was not immediately familiar. My cane sofa had been flung against the cabinet and lay on its side, spreadeagled across the floor. The cabinet had crashed to the ground, its doors flung open, its contents dispersed about the room. All smashed, my pretty things, beyond repair – the earthen water jars, and clear blue vases Sophie gave us on our wedding day, the crystal glasses, my figurines. Only my collection of mazurkas had escaped the young men's anger, systematically deployed.

At my feet lay the photograph of André with his sisters. The three girls sat on the grass, Angeline in the centre smiling her smile of the damned. No, that came later. Her brother standing behind her, one hand brushing nonchalantly against her jet black hair. I picked it up. The glass had shattered from a single blow, trapping all four within its splintered web. A fragment pierced my thumb, no pain but blood welled slowly from the cut and sank between the glass.

Fear ate at my soul. I knew what I must do and leaving Eveline to clear away the mess I telephoned the mayor whom I tracked down eventually to a department in the Ministry of Works.

Gonstran confirmed that Jouvé and his associates had been released at approximately 12.30 p.m. that day, Monday, the 28th of April, after having passed an uncomfortable night in police custody during which they were doubtless subjected to a certain amount of rough treatment.

'Why were they released? Surely with David Taverner's evidence . . .'

'No, Madame. The police assure me that Jouvé has nothing to do with the kidnap of your niece.'

'We'll see about that. With his background he was an obvious candidate.'

'He had an alibi.'

'We all have those.'

'Jouvé's was real,' said Gonstran. 'He was with a woman at the time of the kidnap. She came forward late this morning when word of his capture got round. Apparently the fellow had remained silent about her. We might never have known.'

I suggested to Gonstran that the woman's story was probably make-believe. Females who consort with the likes of Jouvé are little better than pickpockets and whores – their evidence can be discounted. Gonstran was silent, then said quietly that the woman was his daughter, Francine. I wished I had kept my peace.

There was no other way. With trembling fingers I dialled the number of the Chief of Police and requested his immediate attendance. He wished to know my business. I said it could wait until he called. When I hung up I remembered Poincaret at the bottom of the steps and had him removed.

The Commissaire did not trouble to appear in person and sent instead a subaltern, Captain Aguirre, a young and ambitious Martiniquais from a well-connected family. We talked in André's study which had been spared the devastation of the *Santanistes*. I told him of my visit to Claude and how I had returned home to find Agnès in the arms of Jouvé and the others who had destroyed my furniture and left their mark upon the wall. I omitted any mention of Poincaret. Aguirre recorded all this in his notebook, plainly unable to make much sense of the tale.

When I had finished he said, 'Madame, I'm sorry but you're wrong. Edouard Jouvé has been exonerated. He was not involved in your niece's disappearance.'

'Don't you see, you're confusing events on different days.'

Aguirre re-read the notes he had made. 'Correct me if I've misunderstood. What you're saying is this. Your niece disappears early on the morning of the 25th of April. You receive no word from the kidnappers. They make no offer for her release – to you at any rate – and you've no idea who they are. On receipt of certain evidence, now disproved, we pick up Edouard Jouvé for questioning and release him when we're convinced of his innocence.'

'There's no such thing as innocence.'

'That may be. Three days after the original kidnap your niece turns up quite unexpectedly and immediately disappears again. You suspect Edouard Jouvé . . .'

'I don't suspect. I know. I saw him with my own eyes.'

'So you say, Madame. It seems your niece . . . She has a habit of getting kidnapped, does she not?'

His comment stood half-way between a question and a statement. I realised my folly in thinking the police could help me. They cannot hand out parking tickets without causing a riot. I accompanied Aguirre down the steps. He said politely, 'I think you should go away for a few days. You look in need of a rest.'

'Go away . . . Where? On this island you cannot "go away" anywhere.'

A faint groan from the outhouse told me that Poincaret

needed attention. Aguirre must be hard of hearing because he did not stop to investigate.

Poincaret struggled to his feet as I opened the door. His pallid skin was caked with blood and incipient bruises. I had ordered a taxi and sat with him until the car arrived, saying he should speak to no one about what had happened. The police had already been informed and would look for Jouvé and my niece. Before he left I gave him money, all I had with me, and when he protested that he had not submitted his account I explained that this was extra, a form of compensation for his pains.

The rest of that day passed with the timelessness of a dream. Towards evening I called in at the church where a woman from the town arranged flowers on the altar and a group of choir girls practised in a corner. Father Thomas bustled over as soon as he saw me to enquire whether I had any news. No news, at least none that I cared to mention.

Father Thomas said, 'It's time for confession. Have you come . . .'

I declined, wishing no intermediaries before God or men.

'If you will excuse me then . . .' He gave me his plump hand and disappeared into the confessional box where only his feet were visible under the curtain.

I sat in the back row, listening to the choir girls who sang a line of their psalm over and over again: *But as for me, I will walk innocently: O deliver me and be merciful unto me.* Their clear voices rang out under the bell tower, a magnificent sweep up to the high notes on which they faltered, broke off, laughed. I am certain these black girls are better Christians than I: their faith gives them joy. When they fell silent, at last I began to pray.

Reine des Anges, Reine des Patriarches, Reine des Prophètes, Reine des Apôtres, Reine des Martyres, Reine des Confesseurs, Reine des Vierges, Reine de tous les Saints, priez pour nous. Reine conçue sans le péché originel, Reine du très saint Rosaire, Reine de la paix, Agneau de Dieu, qui effacez les péchés du monde, ayez pitié de nous, Seigneur . . .

The girls began a new hymn to their Lord. I wanted to cry, it was such a beautiful melody. And then I made my wager with God. Bring back Agnès, I swore, and I will make the only sacrifice of which I am capable: I will renounce my poet, Claude Arturo Cerda Santiago, and remain for ever in these lands, exiled from the man I love. Just bring her back and I will keep my word.

The girls disappeared. The shuffling of feet outside the confessional told me I was not alone. I waited for some sign that God had heard me and though none came – miracles are not immediately forthcoming – I knew that He had heard me. Father Thomas found me on my knees, repeating my litanies with all the fervour of a convert. Very gently he helped me to my feet.

'Such troubled times,' said the good man, shaking his head at the pity of it all.

'Father, if we do wrong without meaning to, is that a sin?'

'Only God can judge our hearts.'

'That doesn't help me. What I mean is . . . If the consequences of our actions are different, very different, from the ones we intended, are we responsible?'

'We are always responsible.'

'Even for living?'

He took my hand and I regretted my intemperance.

The house was calm when I returned, and empty. Eveline had removed from my sitting-room the broken furniture so that it looked shockingly bare, its only ornament the photograph of André and his sisters in a glassless frame. This was the room of someone who is leaving, who recognises suddenly that strangers may walk here afterwards, may call it home, and that one's residence is always temporary. The starkness of that shuttered room brought me close to tears.

Eveline was equally subdued. She served me quietly at dinner, apologising for the plain white crockery and coarse glassware as if she were to blame for the destruction that had taken place. I heard her moving in the kitchen, restlessly, and for once longed to hear her singing but none came.

The ring of the telephone broke into my reflections. It was David Taverner in a rare, communicative mood. He had heard of Jouvé's release and though it meant we were no closer to finding Agnès, a weight of guilt had lifted from his shoulders. I let him talk. When he noticed my silence he asked if anything were wrong. Perhaps I was too brutal with him. We cannot always be kind and generous to others. You see, I had made the final connection. I was to blame for everything: I had given Gonstran Taverner's paper which led to Jouvé's detention. Jouvé, who was beaten for a crime of which he was, at the time, innocent, had come to my house to vent his anger, had found the girl and in revenge had taken her. The noose of complicity tightened round our necks and soon we would be strangled.

15

THE NEXT day Claude called with his daughters, the little girls of whom he had spoken so often that I knew them as intimately as he. They had become part of my family along with Gustave, André and Maryse, the relatives by birth and the others we choose. Whether I would like them was not a question I considered for a moment. They peopled my universe and had already entered into my private conversations.

I was badly prepared for reality. Claude had shown me a single photograph dating from the time he lived in Venice with their mother. The twins sat on his knee, plump, dimpled and naive, and I had forgotten to compute the passing years. A car drew up and Claude opened the doors with the brisk formality of a chauffeur. The girls climbed out gracefully and linking arms the three advanced towards me, Claude in the centre flanked by these remarkable women who towered above him by almost a head. They were not what I understand by 'little girls'.

'May I present my daughters,' said Claude. 'They came last night, very late. I waited at the quayside. They want to meet my friends. I brought them here as fast as I could. How we shall love each other – my daughters, myself and you, Alicia.' Barely containing his emotion he translated this speech into Spanish and the twins looked as unconvinced as I did.

The woman on his left – Isabella – had an ice-cold Nordic look about her: fair hair brushed back from her face, perfect aquiline features, a manner at once correct and utterly composed. She chilled me to the bone. Rosa, by contrast, had dark curly hair, almost black, and pale skin dotted with freckles. She hopped like a sparrow from foot to foot, never still for a moment, and in her own way disconcerted me just as much as Isabella. We shook hands – Isabella languidly, Rosa with a quick little bob – and as we went up the steps I told Claude of the visit from the *Santanistes*; how Agnès had come and gone.

'What, she was here, yesterday?'

'When I came back from your house. The *Santanistes* were already inside. I couldn't stop them. They had a gun, Taverner's gun – the one he gave to Agnès.'

'Where had she been all this time?'

'Out there somewhere. I don't know. I never spoke to her. They carried her off. She was screaming.'

'You should have called me.'

'What could you do? The police came . . . They didn't believe me.'

'Don't worry, Alicia. The girl can look after herself. She's come back once. She'll come back again. Look on it as an omen. Why shouldn't the police believe you?'

'They said the *Santanistes* were innocent.'

He did not seem particularly disturbed by my news and I resisted the uncharitable thought that he looked on Agnès as a surrogate daughter, no longer needed now the real ones were here. He was none the less shocked when he entered my sitting-room and saw its emptiness.

'They did this, the *Santanistes*?'

'Before they took her. They were angry. You see, the police had questioned them already. They were beaten, I think.'

Claude looked around the room, shaking his head. 'They are vandals. Barbarians. To destroy all this . . . You know I loved your room, Alicia, from the moment I came here . . . It gave me peace.' He relayed the story to his daughters and Isabella tendered her sympathies.

'Never mind,' said Claude more brightly. 'I have something for you. The girls brought it. I asked them to. Oh, you can't know how happy I am, now they are here. We talked all night.'

He disappeared to the car and was gone several minutes. I invited the girls to sit down, which at least they understood. Isabella inclined her head with the grace of a countess while Rosa chattered to her sister, picking at the fabric of her chair with long, white fingers. I smiled until my cheeks ached with the strain.

Claude returned with a large parcel which he handed to Isabella who gave it to Rosa who gave it to me. It was heavy and I nearly dropped it on the floor. Claude came to my rescue and together we carried it to the table. The parcel was wrapped in silver paper with a card that read: *to Alicia de Ste Croix with regards from Rosa and Isabella Cerda.* I recognised Claude's handwriting.

'It's not the first present you've received,' said Claude, making one of his formal Spanish bows. 'My love . . .'

'That's all I ask. You shouldn't have done this.'

'*They* did it,' he replied, a little untruthfully.

It was the most beautiful and at the same time frightening present I have ever received. The silver paper concealed a cardboard box sealed with strong tape which required Eveline's help in locating the scissors. She was busy in the kitchen so we had to wait a few moments. Claude poured us drinks and after a toast – to happiness – we engaged in painfully stilted conversation, each remark channelled through Claude because the twins and I did not possess a common language.

Isabella sat on the sofa, her legs crossed decorously, and said that from her brief acquaintance the island seemed a 'pretty spot'.

'From Isabella, that's praise indeed,' said Claude.

'Please say I'm grateful for her compliments.'

'She's pleased you're pleased,' he said after a short exchange, beaming. Rosa asked if there were many indigenous species of birds.

'Birds? I expect so. I really don't know. The parrots have gone . . .'

'She collects their eggs, don't you Rosa?' It seems the girl had several hundred.

'I'm sorry. Tell Rosa I know so little about birds. There are plenty of insects.'

Rosa did not, however, collect insects. She walked around the room, stopping in front of the photograph of André with his sisters. She laughed and said, through Claude, 'Who's that funny little man? The one with the moustache.'

I stiffened. 'That was André, my first husband.'

Rosa giggled and spoke Spanish to her father.

'What did she say?'

Claude smiled indulgently. 'She asked how many others you had had.'

At last Eveline produced the scissors and I finished opening the box. Even now I remember the shock that went through me as I stared at the head of a woman, half a metre in height, carved out of stone.

'Parvati,' said Claude, 'the goddess. One of Shiva's wives.'

The face had full, sensuous lips and wide open eyes which, because they lacked pupils, seemed to stare inwards at her soul. Eveline saw at once what I had seen and crossed herself hurriedly. Claude looked at the pair of us then back at the goddess placed on the table, who smiled to herself, wickedly. He started. 'I had no idea . . .'

'How long have you had her?'

'The goddess? Full thirty years or more. So that's why I knew her. I thought she came from dreams.'

'Who? What do you mean?' I wanted to take his hand but could not, in front of his daughters. Isabella watched me with the slit eyes of a cat. Deserted by speech, Claude pointed at the statue. Rosa, quiet for a moment, looked quizzically at her father then at me. I quelled my inner fear. The head of the goddess Parvati, who came from Indo-China and was supposedly a thousand years old, had a look about her which was pure Agnès. The night she sat at the head of my table in Angeline's wedding dress, a smile of triumph playing in her eyes, so regal and composed, while we paid court, her servants. Claude raised his glass. The twins followed his example. I wanted to break her face on the wall.

It was gruesome. The rest of their visit had to be endured, somehow. The twins talked merrily with Claude while I took refuge from the statue's harsh, unblinking eyes.

'Claude, where did you get her?' I asked, interrupting their conversation. Isabella turned her head and glared.

'The goddess? In Tonkin. Hanoi, in fact, though the city

was different then. Charming place. Full of lakes and pretty girls. Dying, of course, but if you didn't listen to the guns . . . I lived in Batavia at the time. I told you this, I'm sure.'

'Yes, but you never said what you did.'

'You must appreciate, I was a very young man. I worked for an import-export emporium.' He laughed. 'I wasn't very good at trade. They sacked me soon afterwards. Or maybe I left. I can't remember the details. They wanted to set up an office. In Hanoi. To buy from the families who left. For a song, I think you say. A pretty bloody song. I hadn't the heart for it.'

Isabella, ignoring me completely, said something to Claude which he answered at length. Rosa joined in occasionally as she danced around the room.

'Claude, I asked you about the statue. She . . . frightens me. That smile . . . It says she knows something we don't. I can't explain. Look at her.'

'I think she's beautiful. Like all their women. Delightful. They filled my nights with laughter. In my head, I mean,' he added hastily.

'I know she's beautiful. Only . . .'

'She was never at home in South America. And she'd been travelling with their mother,' said Claude, indicating the twins. Rosa had picked up the photograph of André again and pulled a face at him.

'Their mother? This gets worse and worse. Doesn't she object to your giving her to me?'

'Marguerite? She fell under a train, in Patagonia. Well, she didn't fall, exactly. She jumped. She was always highly strung. I give her to you, Alicia, my little khmer goddess. So what? She'll be happy in your jungles. They'll remind her of her homeland. Do you know, in the three weeks I spent in Hanoi I didn't buy a thing.'

'Except for the goddess.'

'Not even that. At least, I didn't pay for her. I found her on the day I left, in a curio shop near the Métropole. Very second-rate. She stood in the window. That smile . . . Yes, she does have a secret, and her queer satisfaction. She quite enchanted me. I knelt in the street and told her how sick I was of it all. You think me mad, no?'

'Not at all. I have those conversations myself.'

'With stones? I always thought you . . . sensible. As I stood up to leave, half the street blew away. Someone planted a bomb. I would have gone too, if I hadn't talked to Parvati. I knew I had to have her, after that. A kind of charm. I went inside and spoke to a very old man. He was deaf, or stupid. Cupped one hand over his ear in salute and said *oui, mon capitaine*, to everything. It was devilishly awkward. I couldn't work out the price. In the end I just asked if I could take her. *Oui, mon capitaine*, he said, so I did.' Claude grinned. 'That's robbery too, but she'd saved my life.' He reflected for a moment, 'You know, I went back there some time ago. As a guest of the government. I didn't tell them I'd been in trade. The Métropole had changed its name, the city too, and all the pretty girls were gone. It was rather dull, really, although I have the greatest admiration for their leaders. Fate gives them wars and famines, the most unspeakable butcheries, and what do they do? They smile.'

'As they doubtless smiled when they crushed us at Dien Bien Phu.'

'You must allow them their victories. Your empire was already dead. You didn't read the signs. So you sent heroes to fight against ideas. Heroes never win any more, Alicia. Believe me.'

He pressed my hand warmly. Isabella gave a muted sigh. 'Take my statue, Alicia, in memory of me.'

'I don't know how to thank you.'

'Then don't. Remember she cost me nothing though she gave me life.'

I watched him walk across the room. He knelt before the goddess as he must have done all those years ago and placed both hands sensuously about her face, running his fingers across the polished stone. I needed air. We should not witness such private obeisance. Saying I must attend to matters in the kitchen I slipped out by the back door, into the white, midday heat. A neighbour's dog wandered drowsily over the lawn, panting, and disappeared in the shade at the other side. No movement, except the shimmering of light. One of the girls laughed, Rosa probably, in a way that announced she felt quite at home. The sound of foreign conversations. Strangers had come and I was outside the door.

The telephone rang. Eveline went to answer, banging the kitchen door after her. She found me escaping to the bathroom.

'That man for you, Madame,' she said disapprovingly. 'The one who came yesterday. He found Mademoiselle Agnès.'

'Poincaret? What does he want?'

'Didn't ask, Madame. None of my business,' she added bad temperedly.

I took the call in the passage, turning away from my guests. Poincaret wished to know if it were convenient to call.

'I'm sorry, I'm busy. Is it very important?'

'Hard to say. It's a new development. My assistant has filed another report.'

'Max?'

'No, the other one. Jacques. It concerns Señor Cerda.' Poincaret's speech was slurred, I hoped because of his beating rather than drink.

'You should tell me now, in that case,' I said quietly.

'As you wish, Madame. It seems he has a mistress. Jacques is certain of the fact. He's seen the pair himself and everyone's talking of it.'

'I suppose you have a description.'

He flicked through some papers. 'Here we are. Aged between fifty and fifty-five. European. Small, darkish brown hair, neatly dressed with a particular fondness for flowered prints.'

I glanced towards Claude, engrossed in conversation with his daughters. 'You have no idea who the woman might be?'

'Jacques doesn't say.'

'And he can't put two and two together.'

'I don't follow.'

'I'm the woman your assistant dares to insult in this way.'

'Please forgive me. How dreadful . . . I never thought . . .'

'What you think is your own affair. Your services are no longer required.'

'But Madame, there are a number of loose ends.'

'There will always be loose ends.'

He coughed, a particularly unpleasant noise. 'In the circumstances, I might feel compelled to go to the police and tell them everything.'

'That won't be necessary. Captain Aguirre has called already and I have identified the kidnappers.'

'May I ask . . .'

'No. You're no longer involved.'

My hands were shaking as I replaced the receiver. Isabella glanced at me quickly. She has eyes in the back of her head. Claude talked to Rosa, his face glowing with pride and pleasure, obviously unaware of my distressing conversation. The love a father bears for his daughters is very splendid. I wished I could share his sentiments.

They went after we had eaten a simple meal. I was secretly

pleased that Isabella left most of her food untouched and was less than discreetly criticised by Eveline. Claude said she was seasick. Isabella disliked me as much as I disliked her and Rosa remained oblivious of my existence. On his way out Claude shook his head at the goddess and remarked again on her resemblance to Agnès. This was the only reference he made to the girl and I knew that neither I nor Agnès was any match against his daughters.

Eveline skirted around the statue, glowering to herself and murmuring deep-throated incantations. 'It's not right,' she said, 'not right at all. She'll bring us bad luck.'

'Nonsense, Eveline. She's only a stone.'

'Don't you believe it, Madame. I always knew Agnès would return.'

'And so she will. The police are looking for her.'

'A woman told me. But there's plenty she left out. She didn't say Agnès would come back like this,' she pointed at the goddess, 'turned into stone.'

'Stop it, Eveline. I won't listen to your tales.'

'You shut your ears. That's what.'

'Go away.'

'Oh, I'll go away. Eveline'll go right away. It won't change a thing. Not a damned thing.'

'Pull yourself together. This is ridiculous. My friend brought me a present . . .'

'That's not all he give you. Mark my words. You blind too?'

'Get out at once.'

She stopped at the door, saying her rosary and breathing heavily. 'He give you the evil eye, that's what he give you.'

I looked at the goddess and knew exactly what she meant.

16

EVELINE SEES the evil eye in everything these days which I take as a metaphor for her more general dissatisfaction with the state of affairs. This morning she announced her intention to leave my employment. I hope she changes her mind. Having been well served for many years I have come to rely on her, though the departure of Yvette is to be welcomed. The child becomes more savage with each passing day.

When I got rid of the goddess – which I gave to the Englishman just before he left – I hoped that life would return to normal. Not at all. Placing her hands firmly on her hips Eveline declared that though the statue had gone, it had left its eyes behind. Her logic cannot be bought.

I refrained from telling Taverner that I had myself received the statue as a gift. It is ironic that the two men I have ever loved should give me stones which I possess no more.

Agnès would see in that a sign, of one thing or another. Taverner will look after the goddess well. She will become part of his baggage like his grandfather's pistol which he had given to Agnès and which was later returned by Captain Aguirre. My niece was holding it when she died.

The man is to be pitied as much as any of us. He loved her, and though I wished he did not display his emotions so openly, one had to admire his quiet strength in adversity. His newspaper demanded his return, much as Gustave had mine, and he did not care any more. They could shout till they were blue in the face, threaten all kinds of retribution, cut off his expenses, do anything they pleased. He intended to remain on the island until Agnès was found.

I thought it might be Taverner who had fed my niece the *ragoût* of political notions thrown together in her letter to the authorities which was printed in *France-Antilles* and caused such a stir among my compatriots. He swore he had nothing to do with it and that she was ignorant of even the first principles of revolution. None of us, I suggested, knew much about those, certainly not the Chief of Police who visited me himself with the text of Agnès's message so that I might authenticate the handwriting. The script was unmistakeable. The same scrawl that covered page after page in her diary. The same adolescent trampling of accepted beliefs.

Agnès believed in the legitimate struggle of the oppressed against puppet regimes and metropolitan racketeers. She believed in the justice of that glorious day when white races everywhere will be swept aside by the purity of black hatred. She believed she had been misled by her baptism and born of the wrong race at the wrong time. She believed the day had dawned for the dispossessed to snatch back their birthright, like fire from the gods. She believed that the hearts of white men were black and the souls of black men white. She believed in a lot of other things besides, notably innocence, dignity, and death. Or so she said. I think she made the whole thing up, either because she was terrified by the men who held her captive or because she was angry that we had, each one of us, betrayed her.

I hate the sunsets. I'm alone and frightened and nobody cares. They spy on me, play with me, tear me apart and then abandon me.

'She's just a child,' I told the Chief of Police, after reading Agnès's letter. He has a crewcut, which ill-becomes a Frenchman, and an ample belly at which I could not help staring, awestruck.

'How old, exactly?'

'Twenty-one.'

'Hardly a child, Madame. She may have been forced to write such a letter, in which case she is innocent. Or she means precisely what she says, in which case she is guilty. Either way, it can only bring trouble.'

All this talk of innocence irritated me. I asked what he intended to do next. He said it was a matter for the Préfet but the authorities had to ensure the maintenance of law and order at all times.

We were still discussing the problem when the telephone rang and I was forced into the one conversation I had been dreading: Gustave called from France, having just received my telegram. He and Marie-Louise had spent the previous week in Verdun, making the final preparations for my house, and had found the telegram on their return to Paris. My letter had not yet arrived and was anyway badly out of date, especially its misplaced optimism. I explained as best I could that Agnès had been kidnapped and that following the receipt of a communication from her she was suspected of sympathising with her captors.

'That's ridiculous, Alicia.'

'Of course it's ridiculous, but try convincing anyone . . .'

Gustave insisted that I read her 'communication' over the telephone.

'That's not my daughter,' he said emphatically, as soon as I had finished.

'She wrote it.'

'I see. Who is in charge of the investigation?'

Gratefully I passed over my brother to the Chief of Police who tried to elicit information about Agnès's background: her friends, her political beliefs, the company she kept, in a manner which left Gustave clearly outraged. After he had rung off I was questioned about the fact that Agnès had disappeared not once but twice. I said it was quite possibly a mistake, a view he summarily dismissed on the grounds that such heinous crimes were never unpremeditated. Like all the rest he entertained his theories.

Claude called that evening but did not stay long. He had taken his daughters for a drive in the north and the girls were tired by the heat and the twisting roads. They remained in the car. He reminded me of Madame Ségovie's soirée the following night, at which he was to give a public reading of his poems. I said I could not possibly attend and had anyway heard most of his work already.

'There are some new ones. Please come.'

'I can't, with Agnès gone.'

'It'll distract you.'

'I need more than distractions.'

'For my sake . . .'

I relented when he suggested that my presence would give him the greatest happiness as he would know he had at least one friend in the audience. Before leaving he kissed my hand in full view of the Amazons and I was reminded of the bargain I had struck with God in the church.

I went to Madame Ségovie's evening, which was a mistake but I would have discovered sooner or later what happened: the voices on this island are never quiet for long. Although the Mayor claims we speak to be silent, we exchange an inordinate number of words. I had spent the day besieged in my house by a pack of reporters who swarmed as soon as Agnès's letter was printed in the newspaper. Marie-Louise telephoned from France. She said it was impossible to imagine her daughter up in the hills brandishing a machine-gun. As far as I knew, they didn't have machine-guns and anyway, they would not give one to Agnès.

'She can't shoot properly,' said Marie-Louise.

'Precisely,' I replied, which occasioned a fresh burst of tears. Marie-Louise appeared to think that her daughter would have been safer if she had been offered rifle practice instead of piano lessons. There was nothing I could say to calm her, and by the time we said goodbye she was completely hysterical. I hoped Gustave knew what to do.

That evening, when I reached the hall I stepped into the glare of pressmen's flashlights as if I were the star, not Claude. I declined to comment on the latest developments in the Agnès Montfort affair. Claude sat on the platform with Madame Ségovie and the Mayor. I had not realised it was such a grand occasion and wished I had worn my pearls. He waved to me as I was shown to a seat of honour in the front row beside the twins and five young men, very solemn and touchingly handsome, dressed in identical red waistcoats and black berets. Madame Ségovie acknowledged my presence with a slight nod, perhaps because I sat next to her husband, the Secretary-General, and beyond him David Taverner.

I had arrived rather late and the hall – which is used more frequently for dance bands and illicit drinking and therefore smells of rum and perspiration – was packed with earnest young men and women, mostly black though interspersed here and there with the faces of my countrymen. The walls were covered with crudely drawn posters and outside palm trees along the seafront rattled in the wind.

At the appointed hour Madame Ségovie nodded at Mayor Gonstran who took up position in front of the microphone. Adjusting the height, he started to bid us welcome but the only sound to emerge through the speakers was a strident whine. A technician was sent for and Gonstran meanwhile searched through his pockets. Madame Ségovie left the stage to complain to the management, looking darkly at the auditorium as if she suspected foul play. A man in overalls inspected the wiring, re-fixed a few connections and after standing centre stage and counting to himself through the microphone declared the system in order. We sat in an aura of expectancy. Madame Ségovie returned and nodded more curtly at Gonstran.

'My friends,' he started, pausing to check he could be heard, 'we are here tonight to pay tribute to Claude Cerda who, I am sure, needs no introduction.'

He raised his arm to indicate our poet, unfortunately pointing in the wrong direction so that Madame Ségovie, who wore a dress decorated with large red flowers, looked to her left, off stage. Claude nevertheless stood up and bowed to the audience which clapped enthusiastically, all except Isabella and Rosa who treat such honours with disdain.

'Many of you, I know,' said the Mayor, holding up his hands to restrain our welcome, 'will have read his works. My own favourite is a little collection called . . .' He felt in his pockets then said uncertainly, '*Mother of Silence*.'

'Sister,' corrected Claude behind his back.

'What was that?'

'*Sister of Silence*, the title of my collection.'

'Forgive me, of course, *Sisters of Silence*.'

Claude sighed audibly.

'My son, on the other hand, prefers . . .' Gonstran looked at Claude for inspiration, 'the early poems, when you were in exile. What are they called?'

'Which exile?'

'I don't know.'

'Do you mean *A Song to Chile*? Or *Illuminati*?'

'That's right,' said the Mayor unhelpfully.

The audience called out a number of other possibilities. I heard Léopold's voice but could not see him. Claude intervened and suggested it might help if he listed his collections in the chronological order of their original editions. He was given the stage and for several minutes recited Spanish names and dates, then sat down again, looking annoyed. Isabella stiffened at my side.

The Mayor remarked apologetically that he wasn't very good at Spanish which the audience found uproariously amusing. Madame Ségovie called us to order. She should have brought a gavel. I began to feel I might enjoy myself, in spite of everything.

'I believe we have other performers tonight,' said Achille Gonstran above outbursts of sporadic laughter.

Madame Ségovie said, 'Not at all. We must follow the programme.' Claude whispered in her ear. She shook her head and pointed at a paper in front of her on the table.

'Before we begin though,' said the Mayor, 'I would like to say a few words to you.' He patted his pockets a final time. Claude attempted to reassure Madame Ségovie who looked thunderously at Gonstran.

'It concerns the disappearance of Agnès Montfort . . .'

The hall fell silent at a stroke. I felt a pain in my breast.

'There are several stories circulating . . .' Gonstran began, then stopped.

'Get on with it,' muttered a voice from behind.

'The newspapers . . .' said Gonstran, 'we shouldn't believe everything we read in the newspapers.'

A pressman, standing below the stage, said loudly that he felt personally insulted. He turned to the audience for approbation and was clapped and whistled by some of the more rowdy elements.

'You will have read this morning a letter from Mademoiselle Montfort, in praise of revolt . . .'

'Revolution,' said Claude.

'Can't read,' yelled a voice from the back, amidst muffled laughter.

'The question is . . .'

Another voice called, 'Get him off.'

'Who wrote it? That's what I want to ask.' Gonstran looked around him. 'I assure you that everyone will be brought to justice, whatever the colour of their skins.'

He stepped forwards, out of the direct line of the microphone. I struggled to hear his words above the catcalls of the audience.

'She was wrong, you see,' he appeared to be saying, 'about black hearts and white souls. We are misled by appearances . . . I don't know if I'm making myself clear.'

The catcalls increased in volume.

'What is the colour of my heart?' he called in desperation.

'Red,' shouted a wit in one of the front rows – we were the only ones who could hear a word the Mayor said – and pandemonium broke out once more. Isabella spoke to the young man on her right. I think this little group was alone in being untouched by the Mayor's extraordinary performance. Gonstran sat down abruptly beside Claude and

Madame Ségovie. The latter walked determinedly to the microphone and quickly subdued us. When a voice called out, 'that white whore' she turned on her invisible interlocutor and told him to restrain himself or she would throw him out. The woman was in her element and I had to admire her skill in bringing to heel such an unruly crowd. Briskly she offered Claude her own words of welcome without prompting from her mentor: the books he had written, the revolutions he had glorified, the honours he had humbly received. The local newspaperman scribbled despairingly throughout. I had not realised one half of Claude's achievements. She spoke for a full quarter of an hour during which time she mentioned her husband, the Secretary-General only once, and then obliquely. When she came to the end of her speech she announced a change in programme. We would start with some songs.

'They are not ordinary songs. And they correspond well with our theme. Monsieur Cerda,' she said, turning to Claude, 'would you care to introduce . . .'

'My friends,' he said simply, beckoning to the front row. With one accord the young men in black berets and red waistcoats stood up and marched to the stage, bowing at Isabella and Rosa as they passed. They stood before us in a row, these five young men from Chile with their mien of latter-day conquistadores, each one indistinguishable from his companions, the same stance with the head thrown backwards, the same clean-shaven chin, the same tilt of the guitar. One of their number stepped forward and bowed deeply. 'By Victor Jara,' he said, 'his last.'

From the moment the sound of their guitars broke into the sweaty stillness of the hall my heart was lost. I had no idea such joy resided in revolution, such happiness and hope, and though they sang of exile and privations they asked us to rejoice, not mourn. Tears flowed down my face.

These fine young men, so handsome and brave, were the sons I should have borne.

Between songs the same young man stepped forward to the microphone and introduced his music in halting French, charmingly devoid of grammar. 'A folkdance of my Chilean peoples,' he said proudly. '*Las Cuecas del Pañuelo.*' He stepped back into line then called out, 'This he spreads joy with which our struggles we face. He was composèd by Isabel Parra.'

He nodded to his companions. The man at the end of the row beat his hands on his guitar. Another stamped his feet. A third and fourth attacked their guitars, hips swirling, while the fifth man clapped his hands. Then the intricate pattern of their voices overlaid the insistent rhythms, lifting up our hearts so that even Ségovie by my side tapped his feet on the floor and several people behind me were crying quite openly.

It was an unforgettable evening. They sang about death in the stadium, under the starry skies. About the Teoponte guerillas. About a number of other guerillas with unpronounceable names. About the pine trees and penguins of their native land. ('I think you have not penguins here, okay?') About rich and greedy *latifundistas* and simple-hearted *miristas*, saviours of the poor. About agricultural production. (You would never have guessed.) About fascism and death.

One song I remember in particular. It was called *Mr President. El Presidente.* Perhaps it was the young man's favourite too because he told us in execrable French how the peasants journey across the plains and the cold, hard seas, practising a speech they will deliver to the President when they reach his palace. The refrain still rings in my head: *Why did you take away our freedom, Mr President, tell us that? To save you from yourselves, my children, to lock you up and set you free. We must be very strong children, Mr President, to give you such terrible fear.*

Of course when they stand before the President – a very small man on a very large throne, dressed in uniform, before portraits of all the other presidents in all the other uniforms – they have forgotten what they wanted to say. No matter. They are glorious in defeat.

We clapped the five young men, how we clapped. People stood on chairs and demanded immediate encores. Claude was invited to join them in a poem, the one in which the world blows up. He spoke to the guitars as one would to a woman, softly, caressingly at first, his deep voice gaining strength as the music wavered like a flame until the sound of their guitars merged with the pitch of his voice into a single cry which grew louder and more intense then broke off abruptly to leave us with the echo of a flute that spoke of lost dynasties and Spanish dreams. The duet was ecstatically received.

Before the last song the young man smiled for the first time. 'My guitar,' he declared over the opening bars of the music, 'he not is for sale.' The music grew louder, stamping its beat on our hearts. 'He is belonging to the people,' he said fiercely and then, 'he die with the people.' Did he mean his guitar or the hero of his song? No one knew. The music lifted up our spirits and we joined in the chorus as best we could as our voices soared in the Antillean darkness.

When it was over the applause lasted a full five minutes. The audience, having wished to savour the heady intoxication of revolution, had been rewarded beyond its wildest dreams. The normally sedate Ségovie jostled my elbows and stamped his feet like a demon. On stage the five young men, chins raised, arms by their side, received this acclaim with complete impassivity, betraying not the slightest hint of pleasure at such a singular triumph. As we clapped and cheered, the young men nodded to each other, turned and marched to one side of the rostrum where they stood with their arms folded while Gonstran fussed about and found them chairs. They sat down. The applause died away.

All eyes turned to Claude who sat between Madame Ségovie and Gonstran, lost in thought. He looked so deeply troubled that I wanted desperately to leave the hall but stayed where I was, knowing that Isabella would never forgive me. Madame Ségovie spoke to Gonstran behind Claude's back. The good fellow stood up, disappeared off stage and returned with a high stool which he placed in front of the microphone, appealing to Claude to come forward. My friend stood up like one in a dream and moved towards the centre of the stage. Gonstran patted the stool at which Claude stared in bewilderment as if he could no longer understand the purpose of ordinary objects. The silence in the hall vibrated with such intensity that I felt sick and faint.

Claude glanced back at the five young men, then at the audience. 'You know,' he started, pointing to his countrymen, 'I have listened to Marcos and Sebastian and Rodrigo and Felipé . . .'

'*Y Frankie*,' added one of the five.

'And Frankie too, of course. I have listened and my heart grew proud that they share my birthplace. In my country we have many fine young men – and women too. You must come one day . . . But what do they sing of?'

He glared at us without pausing for an answer. 'Of war and killing, that's what they sing of. Of the slaughter that goes on each day, each month. They are misguided,' he said, raising his voice. 'Not these, our glorious poets, but the others. The ones who take to the jungle with their manuals of revolution and their machetes.'

The five young men relaxed in their seats under the mistaken impression that Claude was paying his respects.

'Yes, they are fools because war is dirty and cruel yet we shut our eyes to its cruelty. You can't play your guitar on a battlefield. And what do they want with their dirty little wars? A good death, that's what they want, a bullet slap between the eyes and a seat reserved for them among the martyrs. They want to be *remembered*. It never happens like that, never. I know, because I've been there. They shoot themselves in the dark because they're frightened and can't see. They die of hunger and snake bites and treachery. They are rounded up like pigs because they don't have a compass and tramp off the edge of their maps . . .'

He walked to the front of the stage. Rosa and Isabella spoke to each other in rapid Spanish. The rest of us were mute.

'I'm tired of revolution,' said Claude, 'and I've sat on more committees than I care to remember. For the liberation of El Salvador. Against the massacre of my people. For Allende. Against fascism. Always for or against something. Never just committees. I'm sick and tired but what can I do? The tired revolutionary has no refuge on earth. And there's another thing,' he said, pointing a finger at us in accusation. 'Some time ago one of your people came to me in the middle of the night and said he had a problem with history. Hear me out. I've considered his problem and hoped to see him again to tell him my answer. He never came so I'll tell you in the hope that should you meet him, up in the mountains, you'll remember to pass on my message. It's short and very simple. *There's no such thing as history.*'

A woman at the back of the hall hooted with derision.

'History,' continued Claude, ignoring the interruption, 'is one man's way of looking at the past. Nothing more, nothing less. You add together the short-lived victories and everlasting defeats, the kings and conquistadores. You shake them around to discover a pattern that suits you. It may be perfectly logical which does not mean that it is *right*. And now,' he said, glancing at Madame Ségovie who had grown increasingly alarmed at his wild harangue, 'I will recite the fruit of one of my histories. You may call it a love song. Or a battlecry. Or what you will. I call it *Lady of Midnight*.'

I gave a cry of despair and sank my head in my hands. Isabella turned and looked at me in horror as I stood up, tripped over Ségovie's legs, felt Taverner steady my fall. In the aisle I trampled over latecomers who sat on the floor, threshing a hand here, a foot there, stamping out their angry protests which could never drown Claude's sonorous and inexorable inventory of a woman's body, the body of my niece, Agnès Montfort, the *Señora de la Noce* whose shame was broadcast to the world by a man old enough to be her father, who gloried in her defilement, who found orchids in her breasts, lost continents submerged between her thighs. You may call it a love song . . . You may call it what you will.

Léopold blocked my exit. I pushed him aside, into the arms of Christophine whose glasses fell off. She swore at him. He shouted at me. I kicked the man next to him and reached the street which was empty, desolate, and black as if the sky had fallen down. I ran blindly to my car, dropped the key, crawled on the ground, opened the door and started the engine which detonated the silence of the square.

I do not remember the drive home. Eveline came out to the steps and I told her to leave me alone. In my room I sank on to the bed without crying. It was much too late for that. I stayed there for an hour, maybe more, until I heard the sound of a car and, terrified that my tormentor might have come to hound me, I hid behind the door. The noise went away. I had imagined it. I walked downstairs to the sitting-room, tapping my way along the walls. Without a moon the darkness was total. Claude's goddess stood on the table, her wide unseeing eyes laughing at me. As I stared in deathly fascination she smiled, I swear it, her lips moved into a triumphant grimace that spread across her features and curled the corners of her mouth. *You see I've won*, she said softly, mockingly, my moonstone whore, *what you wanted most I stole.*

No, I shouted.

Yes I did. You know it is true ... You have always known.

Like a sleepwalker I glided across the floor, both hands outstretched, wanting to strangle this damnable vestige of Agnès and banish her forever from my home. I could not. I held my hands before her throat and willed myself to touch the cold stone. She was invincible. My hands dropped to my side.

In my room I took the clock Agnès had given me and flung it against the wall so that it shattered as it fell to the floor. Then I picked up a torch and went out into the plantation.

Do not walk abroad when the spirits roam. Fear the strangers you meet in the forest, and the lights that flicker in the hills. Shut your eyes when dogs howl out their hearts in darkness.

They flocked around me that night: the dogs, the lights, the spirits, as I walked without fear through the agitated trees. The torch picked out myriads of flying insects, and serpents spoke to me – if only I could hear. My footsteps crashed through the undergrowth and once or twice I caught their echo but did not stop to investigate, fearing to chase my shadow.

The hurricane shelter stands at some distance from the house, closed in with giant *sabliers*. It is old, the shelter, built in a hollow with windowless walls and a solid door to batten down the wind. Yes, she would have been frightened, my niece, as she huddled here inside the shelter, frightened by noises and discomfort and the nightmare into which she stumbled, an innocent victim of circumstance.

How many times must I repeat that I believe in neither victims nor innocence. Agnès deserved her fate. Willed us to punish her. A spoilt child, greedy for the dreams of others, she took what she wanted and was slapped in return. That is not innocence. She could have had the Englishman, no one else wanted him, but Agnès wanted more. My friend. My poet of the revolution. She went to him early, before I awoke. She went to him late, after I slept. She called in the daytime when he locked his door to me. She opened her legs for him while he swore on Isabella's honour that he loved me. Another lie more bitter than the rest.

Her diary gave it all away. The moment I read that catalogue of filth I knew the voice did not belong to Agnès, a child, a fool. The words were Claude's, the man I loved above all else, above André, more than my pride. She had destroyed my happiness and taught me what it means to hate.

And so I took her. Yes, I alone was responsible for the taking of Agnès and I exult in that responsibility. The girl was a tramp, schooled in the gutters, who brought her whorish habits into my house and resurrected my deepest fears. Destroyed my past and made of Angeline a saint. The two deserve each other and their reputations. Yes, I took her and made her suffer for the pain she caused me, stripped of a future with the man I love. I ordered Léopold to carry out the deed. He knows our ways. He had her taken to the shelter where Angeline debauched my husband's workers and lay with every man who passed her door. Who would have lain with André had he let her. That prison was the only place for Agnès, alone, abandoned, where voices multiply and terror spawns. I made her suffer and I punished her.

What Agnès did with Claude disgusts me utterly. A satyr grappling with a child. Bodies taking pleasure from each other, limbs wrapped in lust . . . the vision fills me with a sickness I may never cure. He offered me love and a new kind of living. He promised me a future and gave me a stone. He took to bed a worthless whore, my brother's daughter, who seduced him with smiles and pretty laughter and offered up her body when he wanted my soul.

The sin belongs to Agnès. I cannot blame my friend. She flaunted her charms at our darkest desires. A siren who corrupted us . . . When your eye is evil rip it from your body . . . This brings me comfort. I am innocent. I trusted the wisdom of my fathers and plucked out the creeping evil from our midst. The evil that was Agnès.

Her death, I never planned her death. The Englishman must take the blame for that. I wanted her gone to discover the truth. I wanted peace and time alone with Claude. I did not want her dead. But Taverner's meddling drove me to the wall. I had to act, there was no other way. He forced my hand. And so I hired Poincaret, another fool. Why do I live among fools? He might, I thought, bring proof of Claude's affections. He might assure me Claude was undisturbed. I never thought that he would find the bitch. Claude said . . . I should beware of wordsmiths. Hope grows, you see, and love is blind to reason. I thought Claude told me Agnès was a phantom. I thought he spoke of happiness and love, our life together in another place, my cherished dreams. *I thought she did not matter*. A fool like all the others. At every step he duped me and betrayed my trust. They mocked me, both of them. Spun me a web of lies to mimic my despair. She taught him this, my niece, a black madonna who now squeals from hell.

Against all odds Poincaret found her. I never meant him

to. He brought her home, into the hands of the *Santanistes* who pulled her screaming from the house and thus avenged my shame. I heard her terror as they drove her away. She saw me and screamed, knowing I could not help her. Would not help her. I stood aside and watched her disappear, out of my life forever to the fate she so justly deserved, up in the hills. A lonely place to die. I took her, and those screams reward my pains. Her death, unplanned, is cause for joy not sorrow. You do not pity vermin when you crush them. She led us all a dance and broke my heart.

I never thought to tell of this, my secret. That I took Agnès. That I alone was to blame. But now my guilt is out I shall proclaim it from the rooftops. String garlands to announce my shame. And dance now she is dead. In future I shall stop my eyes to dreams and my heart to the promises of men. Her death has purified my world and I shall walk alone, knowing all promises are made to be broken, all honour defiled by lust and fornication. Since Agnès never returned I can forget my bargain with God who forsook me, as they did. Fed me false comforts and deserted me.

Bargains. Promises. Lies. I shall regret *nothing*.

A noise outside the shelter. I spun round in fear, thinking Agnès had returned to taunt me. Yvette stood in the doorway. She screwed up her eyes in the torchlight, both arms held tightly behind her back. We stared at each other and then, very slowly, the little girl drew forward one hand. An object glinted in her palm. She smiled as I moved to take it from her. It was the pendant that once belonged to Agnès. I gave the child my hand and we walked together through the darkness, chased by darting lights and the distant roaring of the spirits, and gave each other strength to face the day.

17

THE END DID not come for another three days. More posters of Agnès appeared by the roadside. The Préfet made a number of speeches on the subject of justice, which he equated with the rule of force.

Agnès continued to record her thoughts in a child's exercise book given to her by her captors. This was later shown to a criminal psychiatrist who found evidence that her mind was unbalanced by the strain of her ordeal. He was not to know that the 'notes' are entirely consistent with Agnès's character. Though I have definite views of her morals and her abominable duplicity I have never considered her mad.

This second diary begins on Wednesday, the 30th of April, two days after she had fallen in with the *Santanistes*, and reveals that whatever faults she had, she was resilient, my niece, and desperately brave.

Wednesday

We're camped on a high ridge somewhere to the east of Pelée. I've never been up here in the wild lands among the giant trees and the orchids, and we haven't seen a soul since we left the roads. The others have machetes and hack our path through the undergrowth, upwards, always upwards, so progress is slow. Most of the time we're in the dark, then dazzled by sudden views across the forests.

I feel stronger today and can walk by myself. At first I was quite weak after the shelter, so two of them had to help me and once I was carried on their backs. They say they had nothing to do with all that and I think they're telling the truth. (They also say they don't hold anything against me personally but have been taught to make political capital out of chance events. I fell into their hands and they took me – it wasn't their fault as they had no alternative. Why do I agree with them when it's so obviously against my interests?) If they didn't lock me in the shelter there's only one person who could hate me that much and I feel incredibly sad. It's all a dream, I tell myself, from which I'll one day escape. My fear of the shelter quickly disappeared. It was a quiet place, very still, shut off from the noises of the forest. A woman came to feed me and stayed to talk sometimes though I couldn't understand much. She never smiled and was very polite. We were playing some kind of game with unspoken rules. Near the end she brought me a lamp and started to tell stories like Eveline, but without the laughter. Sometimes I wonder if it happened at all.

At least the forest is real. There are six of us altogether, including me. They won't reveal their names but treat me well and trust me not to run away. There's nowhere to run to in any case. We're very low on provisions and yesterday we cooked and ate a jungle rat. I couldn't bear to watch them skin it. One of the men has a satchel of books which the others try to throw away. He has a tooth missing and an odd sense of humour. Sometimes he talks to me and seems to like me more than the others. I'm surprised not to feel more afraid.

Thursday

The paths are running out. We've advanced a few kilometres and can hear the noise of helicopters and small planes above the trees. Now their leader says we mustn't light any more fires. We're almost out of matches anyway. The rains are the worst of it. They pass several times a day and most of the night so my dress sticks to my skin. I'm virtually indecent but they look the other way. The whole of my body aches, as if the dampness has crept under my skin. In the morning I can barely walk, I'm so stiff, and the others are in no better shape. When we walked through the sunlight steam rose off their backs. Now their leader insists we stick to the shadows. Earlier we passed a crucifix near the summit. A Christ blackened by mildew whose suffering looked strangely out of place in the jungle. One of the men prayed on his knees and the others laughed. I prayed too and nobody laughed at me.

We rested for several hours in the heat of the day. The man with the missing tooth sat with me apart from the others and read from his books, odds and ends of poetry, philosophy and political pamphlets, mostly rubbish. We were talking about poetry when he mentioned he'd met Claude recently and didn't like him at all. Claude was arrogant, he said, and not to be trusted. I remembered the story Claude told me about the lunatic who appeared one night to talk about history. The man called Hector. Or was it Hercules? It must be him, I'm sure, but I didn't say I'd heard about their meeting. Claude was terribly rude and I wouldn't like to hurt him any further. We had an argument about whether Claude was any good as a poet and he wouldn't talk to me for the rest of the day. One of the others who laughs a lot, nervously, declared they're determined to fight to the end. He made me quite a speech, about suffering and death. I talked of Angeline who had also rebelled, in her own way. He wasn't really interested – said I was trying to personalise the revolution. I don't think I have any alternative.

We're all of us armed. The others have rifles and two rusty machine-guns. I was given David's gun when they found it wasn't loaded. I think of him sometimes and wish I hadn't treated him so badly. It's impossible to escape completely any sense of regret.

Friday

Hector/Hercules has forgiven me and read again from his books. He takes them very seriously and has crammed the margins with comments in his own scratchy handwriting. It is clear that I have always belonged to an inferior race. I cannot understand revolt. My race never rebelled except to pillage, like wolves against an animal they have not killed. I belong to an inferior race for all eternity. And then again: On the day of judgment the trumpet of Armstrong shall be the interpreter of the sorrows of man. I wish we'd met in different circumstances. There's so much to learn. He sulked when I refused to show him my writing. He believes that in a just society nothing is secret. I wanted to laugh and imagined him singing the *Marseillaise* to Claude who thought he was cracked. But there is something heroic about him. He slouches through the jungle like a boy on a Sunday School outing – Claude said that too. He's always right but maybe too hard on the rest of us. I don't know what I'm saying. Who am I to criticise?

We've reached a grassland high in the mountains and must wait for nightfall before we can cross, in case they see us from the air. Helicopters are never very far away. In the far distance a bird calls, high clear notes followed by silence. It guides our way. One of the men said it was a *siffleur de montagne*. We hear noises in the undergrowth, animals probably and lizards which sound like footsteps so we're always on guard. We're dirty and tired and cold to our bones but the others seem more frightened than I am. Can this really be the revolution? I thought it would be braver somehow, and more exciting.

Saturday

This is the last will and testament of Agnès Elisabeth Montfort, written on the 3rd of May and witnessed before God. For understandable reasons my captors can't sign their names but I expect my wishes to be carried out if the worst happens, which we fear. To my mother, Marie-Louise Montfort, and my father, Gustave Montfort, I leave all my personal possessions. I love them and hope they won't grieve. To David Taverner, currently staying at the Hôtel des Innocents, Vauclin, I return his gun. He gave it to me for safe-keeping and never intended me to use it. To Claude Cerda I give my thanks. In the short time I've known him he has introduced me to a better world. I wish the contents of my bank account to be handed over to a defence fund for my captors, should that be necessary. There isn't much but it will show, I hope, that I bear no grudges. They've been as kind to me as the circumstances allowed, and haven't harmed me in any way. I believe they are not responsible. From my aunt, Alicia Montfort de Ste Croix, resident of St Antoine, I ask forgiveness and beg her to understand that I never meant to hurt her. I wish her and Claude every happiness and would like her to believe that I love her too, in my own way. Signed: Agnès Elisabeth Montfort.

I hope the end comes quickly. We're running out of food and the nights are cold in the hills. I can't stop shivering and am covered with cuts and sores which fester in this clinging dampness. We talk endlessly about politics and oppression and what we'll do when it's all over. Then we march to another refuge. I've been entrusted with a machete though I'm not very good with it. Today we outwitted a police patrol and one of the men fell sick. We had to leave him behind and now we are five.

The only known communication from Agnès's kidnappers was sent directly to the radio station and broadcast on the midday news, Friday, the 2nd of May. Unlike Agnès's 'notes', their message was lucid and to the point. They demanded one million francs, the release of Aimé Gerville from prison where he is serving ten years for culpable homicide, and a safe passage to the destination of their choice, as yet undetermined. The Préfet, when questioned about these demands, made no comment.

Achille Gonstran called at my house once or twice to give me the latest news. The police had doubled their road blocks and called in the army whose lorries rumbled through the cane fields until it felt as if we lived through a state of siege. There was even talk of sending in the Foreign Legion.

Gonstran was confident that Agnès would soon be released although he trusts the police and the military as little as I do. I asked him why he had mentioned Agnès in his speech of welcome at Madame Ségovie's evening. He must have known that such an intrusion was tactless if not stupid. As I suspected, he had simply forgotten his speech and had spoken of the event which was uppermost in his mind, having quarrelled with his daughter Francine over Edouard

Jouvé whom she threatened to shelter, if she got the chance. Gonstran asked why I had left the evening so early and I let him think that I was taken ill.

'He got a rough ride, your friend Cerda. The audience had expected something to fire the blood. Well, it did, I suppose but in the wrong way. That first one . . .'

'*Lady of Midnight*?'

'They didn't even applaud.'

'It was in very bad taste.'

'I thought you left . . .'

'Furthermore, it was a bad poem.'

'Oh, you know, me – I wouldn't know about such things. Literature is not my forté.'

'Nor Spanish, it seems.'

He laughed then said more seriously, 'Madame Ségovie thinks he's suffering from exhaustion and should see a doctor. Would you speak to him?'

'Why me?'

'He's your friend, isn't he?'

My silence warned him to change the subject. He asked if I had made any plans for the future and if I had considered his advice – that I should pack my bags and leave the island. 'Yes,' I replied, 'I came close to making a decision. I've changed my mind and now intend to stay.'

'That may not be very wise. You know I'll do my best to protect you. Beyond that . . .'

'I understand. But I shall stay. You can murder me in my bed for all I care.'

'Madame, I would never dream . . .'

'Of course not.'

He is a good man who, like he says, will do his best.

It pains me greatly to relate my next meeting with Claude. We were equally determined to raise none of the spectres that haunted us so we talked of everyday events, of the latest Sino-Russian *rapprochement*, of the hurricane that threatened Dominica. The closest we came to staking out our fears was an agreement that the five young men from Chile were 'very splendid'. They had arrived on the yacht with Isabella and Rosa and two of them would – he hoped – provide fine husbands for his daughters. I believe Frankie and Sebastian were his favourties. He must have noticed that I had relegated the head of the goddess to a corner but, like the Préfet, he made no comment.

Gustave and Marie-Louise arrived from France. I met them at the airport after receiving Gustave's telegram. Someone had alerted the press because they turned out in force and for a short time our island woke up to find its place in history. David Taverner was present in his professional capacity. We talked for a time and I was grateful he did not request any particular favours.

I was shocked by the way my brother had aged. He supported himself on the handrail as he climbed down the aircraft steps and Marie-Louise – who looked like Agnès's elder sister – had to attend to the baggage. She took me aside and said that Gustave was on the verge of a breakdown. She seemed very calm. I had not realised that my brother cared so much about his daughter. They refused my offer of accommodation as they wished to remain at the 'centre of events'. If by that they meant the police headquarters I did not wish to disabuse them. We all needed hope. I drove them to Fort de France where they had reservations at the Hôtel Impératrice. Marie-Louise commented on the fine views across the *Savane* while Gustave merely nodded to indicate that the arrangements were satisfactory. I stayed for dinner in the restaurant, relieved that other people's conversations could disguise our silence. At the next table an American family commented on their meal. As soon as we heard them mention my niece's name, Marie-Louise and I talked loudly about relatives to spare Gustave pain. My brother gave no sign that he had heard and I left them making a call to the police who reported no further developments.

Poincaret dropped by without prior warning. He said that he had cornered Léopold who had finally admitted that he had a hand in the first abduction of Agnès.

'What else did he say?'

'Not much. He said that a third party had asked him to arrange for her to disappear, temporarily. He put a couple of men from Guadeloupe on the job. They were to give her a message from your friend, I believe, saying that he wanted to see her urgently.'

'From Monsieur Cerda?'

'Correct.'

'So he had . . .'

'No, Madame, Leópold swears that Cerda had no part in the business though he refuses to reveal the real identity of the "third party". Once the men had got Agnès to the car they held her at gunpoint and blindfolded her. She was driven half-way around the island, a gun in her ribs, then back to the hurricane shelter.'

I asked whether Agnès had suffered at all, in this brief captivity.

'According to Léopold, no. The men returned to Guadeloupe and a woman was hired to look after the girl.'

'A woman of these parts?'

'I believe so. The orders were that she should not be harmed in any way. And then . . .' he shrugged.

'What?'

'You know the rest.'

I asked if he had told anyone about this conversation with Léopold. He shook his head.

'So what do you intend to do now?'

Poincaret crossed his legs and stared at me. He has the features of a small rat.

I said carefully, 'I do not respond to blackmail.'

'Why should you, Madame?'

'Do you expect payment for this . . . information. I thought our agreement was terminated.'

'Shall we say that I spent an extra few days on the case.'

'Two thousand francs?'

'Make it five thousand, Madame. You must admit the price is reasonable.'

I gave him the money, insisting that he sign a statement to the effect that this was his final payment on the Montfort case and that he was no longer in my employment. After he had pocketed the money I asked why he had continued to take an interest in the business, against my wishes. He called it 'professional curiosity'. We shall see.

I was in church when the final assault took place, listening to the drone of Father Thomas's prayers. We had a lot to pray for and the service lasted a good ten minutes longer than usual. They were waiting for me when I came out, Captain Aguirre and his colleagues. As soon as I saw their faces I knew that the worst had happened but stayed chatting on the steps with Father Thomas because until I confronted Aguirre I was saved from the truth. Father Thomas shook my hand and declared that everything happens by the will of God. Perhaps he is skilled at mind-reading because his words implied that I could not be held responsible.

Captain Aguirre and his men stood stiffly to attention as I approached. More handshakes. The man told me what had happened and offered his deepest sympathies.

'You are in charge of policemen,' I observed, 'not storm troopers.'

'We did our best, Madame.'
'As I feared from the start.'
I accepted a police escort and travelled into Fort de France at speed in my silver-grey Citroën flanked by outriders on motorcycles, along the *route nationale*, across the plain of Lamentin, past Chateaubœuf then up behind the town to avoid the traffic, through Terres Sainville and down the rue du Pavé. We arrived in style at the Hôtel Impératrice.
Marie-Louise and Gustave were locked in their room to escape the surge of pressmen in the lobby. The Englishman was absent: either he had learnt to respect grief or he stalked the hills with the others. The manager himself escorted me through the crowd.
'Madame, do you think . . .'
'Did Mademoiselle Montfort join the terrorists . . .'
'A question Madame . . .'
'. . . can we say you're shocked?'
'. . . is Edouard Jouvé responsible?'
'How do you feel?'
'. . . and did you think that it would . . .'
'. . . are the police to blame?'
'. . . unnecessary force . . .'
'The Préfet said . . .'
'. . . come to this?'
'Madame, please, who do you think . . .'
'. . . we understand the army . . .'
'. . . shot Agnès Montfort?'
I turned to face the rabble. They fell silent, notebooks ready. Lights flashed in my face. They stared at me and I was sure they gloated. They had a story while I had nothing. The manager took my elbow and hurried me away. Inside their room my brother was turned to stone. Marie-Louise rose to greet me and though obviously distressed she had mastered her sorrow, perhaps because her husband needed her. After

we embraced she said she wished she had brought something black.

'We cannot be ready for every eventuality.'

'I never thought . . .'

'We none of us did.'

Marie-Louise had prepared herself to identify Agnès's body. Such formalities seemed excessively brutal. We all knew it was her – the police, her family, the press – yet we had to fill in forms for the record. I offered to accompany her. The task was clearly beyond Gustave who had not moved since I arrived.

'No thank you,' she said bravely, 'I wish to spend a few moments alone with my daughter.'

I held her in my arms and wished that I could cry.

When I got home I turned on the television. The Commissaire stood with his hands on his hips, protruding his belly over the flaccid bodies of three 'terrorists' in a heap, peppered with gunshot, arms and legs spreadeagled on the earth, wide open eyes staring at the skies. We are accustomed to such images by now: the victors with their trophies who seem pathetically helpless now they are dead. At least they had had the good sense to leave Agnès out of the picture. One should not gloat over the innocent.

The business was a shambles from beginning to end. No one needed to die. Certainly the terrorists had not planned such a result, they were opportunists like the rest of us though a little less skilful. As Claude would say, the taking of Agnès was a symbol in a world that had suffered too many already, to the point of indigestion. And no one gained from the slaughter. The authorities could claim the restoration of the rule of law but at a cost most of us considered unacceptable.

It took several days to piece together what had really happened up in the hills. The man who fell sick from an unidentified fever, Hervé Gounel, was captured by police after he had been deserted by his comrades. Under questioning he revealed more than was wise and the police were able to deduce Jouvé's likely destination: a ruined look-out post on the Morne des Olives, near the Trace des Jésuites. After he had given away this vital information Gounel was taken to the police station at Morne des Esses where he was improperly guarded. His jailer, a distant cousin, knew him well, after all. Consumed by guilt and self-recriminations, Gounel stole his cousin's gun and shot him through the heart. In spite of the fever he made his way up the mountain, avoiding the roads. What happened to Gounel when he told his colleagues of his treachery will never be known: he was found in a different part of the look-out and may have been executed.

When morning came the combined forces of the army and the police mounted their assault. First a helicopter flew low over the look-out with the intention of dropping smoke canisters on to the terrorists to drive them out like cattle. At the moment of release, Jouvé's gang opened fire and the helicopter pulled away sharply. The canisters landed in the wrong place and rolled into the waiting ranks of armed men in camouflage uniforms who emerged coughing and spluttering to face haphazard bursts of gunfire from the *Santanistes.* One must presume they shot to kill although their aim was poor. As more and more police and soldiers poured out of the smoke to see their wounded colleagues on the ground any idea of surrender or the rescue of my niece was out of the question. The Commissaire is said to have shouted for calm through a megaphone. They fought to the death, evidently.

By the time it was over nine people had lost their lives, five terrorists (including Gounel), three policemen and my niece who was shot in the back. As both sides used the same rifles it is impossible to prove beyond doubt who shot her. The police and the army naturally blame the bandits and as the latter are dead they cannot argue their case. At the enquiry, the official version was upheld. I have my doubts, which I have relayed to the authorities who say that I am entitled to my point of view. In addition, four army officers and six policemen were wounded, none seriously. On receiving the news the Préfet is said to have remarked that it 'could have been worse.' We await his recall to France.

I switched off the television and have only misty recollections of how I spent the rest of the day. Perhaps like Gustave I was turned to stone. I understand the doctor called and probably my neighbours because I remember shaking several people by the hand, something I do more frequently these days. Claude telephoned, and the Englishman, who must have promised to call the following day because he arrived on my doorstep holding a large bouquet of flowers, white flowers, which I passed to Eveline and we sat in the shade of my fine cassia trees which rustled above our heads. Eveline's uncle fussed in the background, tending my now depleted flowerbeds.

Taverner talked of Agnès and his disjointed ramblings were tiresome in the extreme. He remembered the times they had been happy together, in Vauclin and Fort de France and on their journeys around the island. Agnès, he said, had an extraordinary capacity for delight at the freshness and kaleidoscopic beauty of the landscape. He passed over her growing coolness towards him, having apparently forgotten that by the end she refused to speak with him and was never at home when he called.

At last I could bear it no longer. 'You Englishmen,' I said, 'you're all the same. You have the brains of a shopkeeper and the heart of a romantic. So brave and so stupid. You and Agnès indeed . . . Do you know what she thought of you?

How she led you a dance like our blessed spirits? You *shall* not love her.'

I then committed the one act for which I am truly sorry because it was born of malice and the penance ordered by Father Thomas can never repair the harm I caused. I showed him Agnès's diary.

'There is your little innocent,' I said, handing him the notebook with the broken clasp in which she recorded the progress of simultaneous affairs. He read it without a word and his face gave nothing away.

'Well, that's it, isn't it, Madame?' he said when he had finished. 'Black and white. I mean, you can't argue with that, can you?'

'I thought it better that you knew.'

'Quite right, Madame. It's better in the end. And this other man – I presume it's a man – the one whose lady she will be . . . he is . . .'

'My dearest friend.'

Taverner avoided my eyes. He skimmed once more through the pages, his eyes barely focused on her writing, then he exclaimed and, holding up the diary to the light, said, 'There's a page missing – the 16th of April – that was her birthday, wasn't it, the day before the riot?' I nodded. 'Someone has torn it out. Look, you can see the rough edges. Did Agnès destroy it?'

Perhaps my expression gave me away because he turned and asked if I had done it. 'I answer to no one,' I replied. 'But you can tell me something if you will. The night of her birthday. I retired early, remember, and left you dancing. What time did you leave?'

Taverner could not remember the exact hour. It was late, maybe 2 a.m. or thereabouts.

'You were the the last to leave?' I enquired, aware of my palpitating heart.

'Your friend was there. He and Agnès talked on the veranda. I left them and returned to Vauclin. Why do you ask, Madame?'

'It's of no consequence,' I said, 'at least, not any more.'

The man in Agnès's room was Claude, as I had suspected. In her diary she had not given him a name, had written simply that a new world opened up before her eyes, one she was terrified might prove to be a dream and which she must grasp before it slipped away like quicksilver. The magnitude of Claude's treachery, now I knew it for a fact, quite took my breath away and I cursed myself for having seen that look in Claude's eyes, love crossed with yearning, the look my husband gave to Angeline, and for having done nothing to prevent their inevitable union. I saw and chose to look the other way.

We were both lost to thought when the figure of Claude appeared at the far end of the drive. He waved and the two of us stood up to greet him. In silence we mounted the steps and I noted a trail of fat white ants that gnawed at the rotten wood. I would ask Eveline to call the carpenter who should attend also to the cracked tiles on the outhouse roof and the door on rusty hinges which blows open and shut in the wind. Without regular attention my house will be reclaimed by the jungle.

We settled on the veranda, the Englishman attempting to master his emotions which he betrayed through a slight playing of hands on his imaginary piano. He and Claude began to speak at once. Claude laughed. The Englishman said he had just heard about the other man's relationship with Agnès. Claude glanced in my direction and I knew I had no place among the men.

'That's your business,' said Claude to Taverner, a trifle illogically.

Taverner sat very straight in his chair, exercising considerable restraint, 'I phoned you from the airport, when my plane was delayed. You asked if I'd seen Agnès as you had expected her to call. When I found out she'd disappeared I forgot all about that conversation. I never asked myself why she might visit you.'

'She helped in my work,' said Claude, 'supplied translations.'

'And more besides.'

'What I did with Agnès is my own affair.'

'I loved her,' said Taverner quietly. 'Don't laugh. She was important to me.'

'You take life too seriously.'

'Too seriously?' The Englishman's self-control broke momentarily. Like Agnès he was desperately brave. 'Too seriously?' he said again, 'the girl is dead.'

I wanted to intervene but could not. It was right that they should fight over her.

Claude leaned towards the other and said he wished to make it clear that he was not in love with Agnès.

'Then why did you encourage her?'

'I gave her something she couldn't get from you.'

'You've said already you didn't love her.'

'Love, love. You sound like a gramophone record. Do you really believe that love is the mainspring of human action?'

'It's all we've got.'

'You're wrong, my friend, love is often an illusion.'

'What could you offer her,' asked Taverner stubbornly, 'that was better than love?'

Claude opened up his hands. 'Immortality,' he said with a smile.

Taverner looked at him appalled. 'She's bloody dead!'

'That is, indeed, unfortunate.'

'A girl shot in the back and you call it unfortunate? I don't see . . .'

'Could you do as much? It's the young who worry most about the hereafter. They can't believe the world will continue without them. She wanted immortality and I gave it to her in a few simple lines that will sell a million copies in thirty languages, even Yoruba and Serbo-Croat where I am, apparently, a hero of the resistance. She wished with all her heart to be my lady of midnight.'

'And was she?' I asked, joining for the first time this argument between men.

Claude reached for my hand. 'It's not as simple as that, Alicia, you should have learnt that by now.'

I pretended that the hand of mine he held was separate from my body. Claude was not worthy of us, in the end, and I wanted to comfort the Englishman lost in his illusion of love. I remembered the keepers of the fighting cocks who, after a fight is over, slip the heads of wounded birds into their mouths, to suck away the blood. I wished to do the same with Taverner, a brave strutting cock who had fought for Agnès even after death and though he had lost he gained a certain kind of victory, the triumph of an honest man.

'You know, I rather like the Englishman,' said Claude when the other had gone.

I saw Claude only once after that. We went for a drive to places we had never visited together. By a curious coincidence – it was not intended – we found ourselves in Ste Anne, home of the ill-fated *Santanistes*, where we walked along the fine white sands under the palm trees then up along the coast road, past the *cimetière marin*, and on to the sleepy little town drugged in the noonday heat. We drank beer in a bamboo hut by the sea, among a scattering of tourists, a girl in a bright red dress, much too short, and a man who plainly suffered from sunstroke.

Claude was leaving the following day with Isabella and Rosa and the five young men from Chile, downcast because he knew he could never return to his homeland under the generals. He could accommodate but not betray his conscience. They would sail to Mexico where Claude had a number of revolutionary friends. I asked him what he meant, in that case, by his conversation about rooms the day he had proposed to me. He looked stunned.

'Alicia, Alicia,' he said, curling his tongue around my name. 'What are you talking about? Rooms . . . Houses . . . I proposed . . .' He put down his glass and turned to face me.

'You asked which room I would have. You said that Isabella . . .'

'I remember,' he broke in, 'but marriage? When did we speak of that?'

'We sat outside, by your house. You must remember.'

He nodded. 'The light sank behind the hills and it was very lovely. You said . . . What was it?'

'I would take a room at the centre of your house. You asked me.'

He smiled. 'A perfect choice, if I may say so.'

'Then you promised to call for your daughters.'

'But marriage,' he said, taking my hand before I could remove it. 'I would surely remember that.'

He looked at me closely, frowning in the bright sunlight. I looked away. The girl in the short red dress stood up to leave. She dropped her handbag and bent down to retrieve it. Claude's eyes strayed in her direction then quickly back to me.

'Alicia,' he said so softly I could barely hear him, 'you say I asked you to marry me.'

'Forget I mentioned it.'

'What did you answer?'

'Claude, please. Don't be cruel.'

The girl paused at the exit to the café-bar. Her companion put his arm around her shoulder and spoke in her ear. She smiled and looked at us curiously.

'Your answer, Alicia . . .'

He pressed my hand. I shook him off. He sat before me, a wily old fox, and I could bear it no more. I stood up from the table and said angrily that if he had never asked me, I can never have replied. I said other things too that I would rather forget and my anger hung between us as we drove to Salines where we left the car and stood on the sands by the Canal de Ste Lucie looking out at the English island which they say is very backward, very poor. Claude asked quite humbly if he might recite a poem, just a little one, written by Octavio Paz. The words caught in my throat. I could not stop him so he stands in my final memory, a stout little man with his trousers rolled up, saying in his fine Spanish voice, *Si el hombre es polvo . . .*

> If man is dust
> Those who go through the plains
> Are men

Then the storm broke around us so we took shelter under the palm trees, watching shafts of rain beat into the sand while out to sea a rainbow moved gently across the water and I knew in my heart I was damned.

End-Note

The *Jour des Morts* approaches. I shall visit André who has cause to reproach my recent inattentiveness, and take him candles and flowers and remembered conversations. It is the time I fear most, when the abandoned ones return to haunt the living, the ones who have suffered violent death without sacraments or sepulchral rites, wanderers on the face of the earth.

This morning, as I looked out of my window, I wished suddenly that all the leaves had fallen in the night to signal the approach of winter. Gonstran is right, I do not belong here. But where can I go? I have no other country, not now, and am too old to vagabond across the plains. My only link with the islanders is through Angeline's daughter who, as Poincaret discovered, still lives, having been 'removed' shortly after birth. She will be thirty by now and doubtless a fine-looking woman. I often wonder if I see her in the faces around me.

Be that as it may, I have put my house in order, declared a truce with my conscience, tidied away the messy bits and pieces of my life. I help others whenever I can from which I gain my greatest happiness. If only the voices would leave me alone, and the demons which drop by, uninvited. I look for them round impossible corners, like spies, and seek to placate their anger with false offerings. They are stronger than I and infinitely more cunning, forcing me to speak of events I hoped might die with me. My truth for their silence, that was the pact we made – then they callously revoked their part of the bargain. I suppose you cannot expect a devil to play by the rules. But where is the justice of it all?

Strangely enough we all got what we wanted: Taverner a story to repair his fragile reputation; myself the knowledge that Gustave will never dare in future step foot in my affairs. Claude, too, did not leave empty-handed. As no one applauded his efforts he can forget his fame and devote his attention to creating a new language to speak across centuries of silence. Even Agnès achieved her ambition: she passed into folklore. In certain versions of the legend she treads at night in the hills and brings luck to all the travellers who cross her path. They sing songs about her at festivals, about the brave young French girl who called the men to arms. I understand that I appear in these as well, a reference which Gonstran says is most unflattering.

The trouble is that by the end our wishes had altered somewhat. It is better to want nothing so you cannot be deceived.

Gustave and Marie-Louise flew back to France with the body of their daughter. We saw each other several times before they left, all painful occasions, and do not think me hard if I say I was relieved by their departure. I was powerless to reverse the course of events and though I mourned my niece I could not share the depths of their sorrow. But I introduced them to Father Thomas who shed a little light into their darkness. My brother wrote as soon as they returned home, a few lines to thank me for my pains. He sounded incongruously cheerful and ended his letter by saying that he knew I would always treasure his 'little girl' whose courage in adversity shall be a lesson to us all. Since then I have heard nothing although I expect Marie-Louise will write a long letter at Christmas.

Claude wrote to me just once desiring, as he put it, to set the record straight. Despite his angry words to Taverner he swore that Agnès had never been the inspiration for his lady of midnight who was born of his imagination alone. When she had appeared in Angeline's wedding dress it was as if she stepped from his dreams. And when your thoughts take flesh you must reach out for them, whatever the consequences. Though he could not deny their relationship was sexual – and he had therefore betrayed my trust and acted shamefully under my roof – the girl was no more than a temporary aberration which would pass like all the others. He regretted also that I had misread his intentions. It saddened him to cause me pain as he thought of me with respect and gratitude for all my kindnesses. He had always, he said, considered me his greatest friend.

I tore the letter into little pieces. It could be true, it could be false, it did not matter any more. We had all misread his intentions and set in train the sequence of events that led to the girl's murder in the hills, because she was murdered, whoever pointed the gun.

Each of us guilty, but who must bear the greatest share of blame? That was the question I set myself at the beginning, and now I am nearing the end the answer continues to elude me. Perhaps it always will.

Let me start with the Englishman. If he had not wired the story of Agnès's disappearance, nothing would have happened. Jouvé and the bandits would not have joined the band of involuntary martyrs. Apart from Claude and myself, no one would have noticed her absence. No fuss. No story. Certainly no tragedy. After an uncomfortable few days I could have returned the girl to France, as planned. And Taverner gave her a gun. While this may have only tangential significance, guns – even unloaded – command a powerful grip on our imaginations.

Much of Claude's conduct was inexcusable. He dismissed the importance of his affair with Agnès but he lied, to me, to her, to all of us, he bartered with fine words and short-changed us wickedly. Had he acted more correctly my niece would be alive to this day. It is possible, too, that his moonlit conversation with Hector provoked the bandits into a final act of vengeance to prove beyond doubt they were a force with which to reckon. That connection remains unproved, and for the rest I shall never forgive him.

They are all implicated in one way or another: Eveline with her stories; Yvette who roams the forest; Angeline by her example; Léopold who should have kept his mouth shut; Leclerc who stole my stones and Poincaret who blundered across them by chance; my brother Gustave who ignored repeated warnings; the men who took her, and the one who shot her. All guilty. Only Achille Gonstran, Mayor of St Antoine, emerges with his dignity intact, the man who – ironically – says we speak of dignity too often and too emptily. One day I may tell him what really happened although I suspect he has already guessed.

Agnès herself cannot be absolved from blame. Had she learnt to distinguish between fact and fantasy, truth and lies, goodness and evil, she would walk among us still. To play with fire requires a fine sense of timing. One need not be a genius to appreciate the truth of that little maxim.

And what of the part I played in the taking of Agnès? I

fully accept my guilt but plead extenuating circumstances – I was, you must agree, as deeply wronged as Agnès. No, the matter of guilt may never be resolved and it is clear I should have phrased the question differently: not who was guilty, but who suffered most?

The hatred I bore my niece has gone now, purged by her senseless slaughter and the knowledge that Claude made us each his victim. In place of the hatred I have only emptiness and a deep sense of loss: love died with Agnès, and my belief in the goodness of man. I think of her constantly and sometimes catch the echo of her laughter which calls from empty rooms. I never find her, however hard I search, but in my heart I know she has forgiven me, as I forgive her, and the only charity I seek is that of silence.

Now I sit on the veranda and look out over the cassia trees as the light fades. I have taken up watercolours for which I receive instruction from an Italian woman in Fort de France, who declares I am her most promising pupil. I fear she exaggerates but I enjoy my new-found passion. I am happiest with landscapes which I paint largely from memory.

Leclerc called the other day. I have never confronted him with my knowledge of his guilty secret but the minute he dares to display my stones in the museum to which I have become a frequent visitor, I shall demand his head.

Eveline, at least, remains in my employment as her crisis has passed. Yesterday she told me another of her stories. Should you see a funny little bundle poked in the bushes under a silk-cotton tree, steal it when no one is looking: it is the human skin of a *loupgarou*. You will have notched up your first victory vis-à-vis the supernatural. Place it in a large stone mortar, add pepper and salt, sprinkle liberally with herbs and pound it emphatically to pulp. Without its skin the *loupgarou* catches cold and dies of exposure. I laughed heartily and wished my own ghosts could be so easily destroyed.

The light has faded and winged creatures swarm about the lamps. I, too, hate the sunsets and the suffocating emptiness of this island where nothing much happens, *no pasa nada*, beyond the odd disaster or two for which there is always a lone survivor – in this case myself, a woman who chooses not to dream any more. Tonight, after dinner, I shall play my mazurkas one after the other, lively tunes to which I dance when Eveline has left me. They shall not make me grieve. I lead a quiet life now that they have gone, with ups and downs like everyone else but lacking any dramas. I have passed through the fever which bewitches all who remain on this island where we play blind man's buff with ourselves and with each other, and struggle with history; and though I shall remain here for ever I have discarded any notion of belonging. Tomorrow I shall get up early, drink coffee underneath the trees, then take my easel to a quiet corner of my land where I shall paint for most of the morning, and do not be surprised if into the picture I slip the pear trees of my childhood and the grey skies of France.